"What if I stay longer?"

He gave her hair another slow stroke. "Or don't leave at all?" The question brought her blinking awake, as he'd known it would. Pushing upright, she propped herself on an elbow. Her hair fell across her forehead. When she hooked the loose strand behind her ear, he saw her face clearly in the moonlight streaming through the top half of plantation shutters. Saw, too, the question in her eyes.

"We agreed up front that we both need our space, Luis. We discussed boundaries."

"Perhaps it's time to renegotiate those boundaries."

"Why?"

"I want more of you, Claire."

"You have all I'm prepared to give right now," she said quietly. "All I *can* give."

Dear Reader,

As many of you know, Claire Cantwell, code name Cyrene, and sexy Colonel Luis Esteban have appeared as secondary characters in a number of CODE NAME: DANGER novels. I plotted their book years ago, but other projects kept getting in the way. So many readers have asked for their story, though, that I've—finally!—written it. I hope you have as much fun as I did going along on the mission that tested both Claire's skills and her ability to resist Luis's determined pursuit.

If you'd like to see photos of the places and events described in this book, go to my Web site at www.merlinelovelace.com and click on the Travel tab at the top of the page, then on the album labeled Europe '07.

And be sure to watch for the next CODE NAME: DANGER book, coming in 2010 from the Silhouette Romantic Suspense line.

All my best,

Merline

MERLINE LOVELACE

Seduced by the Operative

Silhouette®

Romantic
SUSPENSE

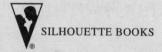

SILHOUETTE BOOKS

ISBN-13: 978-0-373-27659-2

SEDUCED BY THE OPERATIVE

Recycling programs
for this product may
not exist in your area.

Books by Merline Lovelace

MERLINE LOVELACE

A retired U.S. Air Force officer, Merline Lovelace served at bases all over the world, including Taiwan, Vietnam and at the Pentagon. When she hung up her uniform for the last time, she decided to combine her love of adventure with a flair for storytelling, basing many of her tales on her experiences in the service.

Since then, she's produced more than seventy-five action-packed novels, many of which have made *USA TODAY* and Waldenbooks bestseller lists. Over ten million copies of her works are in print in thirty-one countries. Named Oklahoma's Writer of the Year and the Oklahoma Female Veteran of the Year, Merline is also a recipient of a Romance Writers of America's prestigious RITA® Award.

When she's not glued to her keyboard, she and her husband enjoy traveling and chasing little white balls around the fairways of Oklahoma. Check out her Web site at www.merlinelovelace.com for news, contests and information about upcoming releases.

To Marie and Tom and Caren and Mike.
What a wonderful adventure our trip to Prague was.
And thanks for that excursion to the bone ossuary—
who wudda thunk I'd get a whole book out of it!

Chapter 1

"The terrifying dreams started two nights ago."

Dr. Claire Cantwell listened carefully as Nick Jensen, code name Lightning, wheeled his sleek Jag down Pennsylvania Avenue. The warm May weather had brought lunchtime crowds pouring out of the federal buildings that lined the broad avenue. Yet Claire didn't so much as glance at the people crowding into outdoor cafes or lined up at street vendor carts. Her attention remained riveted on the man at her side.

Tall, tanned and tawny-haired, Nick served as special envoy to the president. The title was one of those empty honorifics spun up for a wealthy campaign contributor decades ago. Only a handful of Washington insiders knew the position served as a facade for Nick's real job—director of OMEGA, an ultrasecret government agency whose operatives were activated only at the direction of the president.

One of them had just been activated. Nick had swung by her office a few moments ago on his way to the White House. Claire Cantwell, code name Cyrene, was getting briefed on her mission on the fly.

A psychologist by profession, Claire had made a painful transition into the grim world of forensic psychology and hostage negotiation after her husband's kidnapping and brutal murder almost six years ago. That expertise stood her in good stead during the dangerous and highly secret ops she worked as an undercover operative for OMEGA.

This mission apparently would draw more on her skills as a psychologist than a secret agent. Still trying to assimilate the facts surrounding the president's abrupt cancellation of a goodwill swing through Central America, due to his teenage daughter's terrifying nightmares, Claire probed for details.

"Did they give you any information about the nature of the nightmares?"

"Only that they hit suddenly, late at night. Or rather, early in the morning. Around three or four a.m."

"That's when most dreams occur," she acknowledged. "During REM—rapid eye movement—sleep. That normally takes place in the latter stages of the sleep cycle."

"The girl woke screaming and soaked in sweat," Lightning related. "The first night, the physician accompanying the presidential party thought she'd simply overdone it while touring schools and special events. He gave her a mild sedative to help her sleep. The second night, the visions were evidently so real, so terrifying, that the president decided to bring her home. He's worried sick about her."

"Understandable. She's his only child."

His only immediate family, in fact. John Jefferson Andrews had lost his wife to cancer when he was a charismatic young governor. Since then he'd balanced the demands of his political career against the needs of his daughter.

That much was well-known. What hadn't been made quite so public was that Andrews's party put enormous pressure on him to run for president. He'd turned them down repeatedly, and only threw his hat in the ring after his supporters convinced him Washington needed an infusion of fresh blood.

It did. Desperately.

Andrews's determination to clean house hadn't made him popular with certain career bureaucrats and Beltway bandits, however. He'd taken office in January. Now, just four months later, noisy grumbling could be heard in the halls of congress and various federal departments.

"The president asked for you personally," Lightning said as he pulled up to the first White House security checkpoint. "You impressed both him and his daughter when you briefed them on the emotional and psychological stresses unique to the Washington environment."

"I'll certainly do whatever I can to help, although I haven't had a great deal of experience in adolescent psychology."

The *whap-whap-whap* of a helicopter passing low overhead almost drowned her out. By the time Claire and Lightning cleared the subsequent checkpoints and walked out to the heliport, Marine One was touching down.

The steps lowered and the president emerged first. Lean and fit and boyishly handsome, John Andrews had captured the public's imagination with his energy and obvious devotion to his daughter. Both showed as he turned to help the teenager descend.

Claire studied the dark-haired young woman as she crossed the lawn with her father. Her body language spoke volumes. Shoulders hunched, she kept her head down and avoided looking at the group who'd turned out to welcome home the presidential party. The only sign of a normal fourteen-year-old was the iPod poking out of the pocket of her bright red jacket and the white earbuds looped around her neck.

The president gave Lightning's hand a quick shake before turning to Claire. "Thanks for rearranging your schedule for us, Dr. Cantwell."

"You're welcome, sir." She returned his firm handshake before shifting her gaze to the teenager. "It's good to see you again, Stacy."

The girl nodded and murmured a greeting.

"Your father thought it might help you to talk about what happened during the trip. I'll be happy to chat, if that's okay with you."

The teen lifted her head then, and shocked Claire with the dark circles under her eyes. In a few short days, the smiling, happy young girl who'd waved to photographers before boarding Air Force One had acquired a haunted look.

"I guess."

The president laid an arm across his daughter's shoulders. "Why don't you take Dr. Cantwell up to the living quarters, Stace? I need to go to the office and make a few calls."

"Okay."

Claire started to follow the teen, but caught sight of a familiar figure descending the steps of

Marine One. Her pulse gave a sudden kick and a wry smile tipped her lip.

Colonel Luis Esteban made Antonio Banderas look like something the cat dug up.

She should be conditioned to the impact of his curling black hair, bronzed skin, silky mustache and come-hither smile, all wrapped up in six foot two inches of solid male. She and Luis had worked several missions together. More to the point, they'd been lovers for almost a year now. Between her practice and periodic missions for OMEGA, and his frequent trips back to his own country, they saw each other often enough to maintain the sizzle, but *not* so often that the mere sight of him should send heat racing through her veins and clench the muscles low in her belly.

They'd first met years ago, when he served as chief of security for the Central American nation of Cartoza. In that capacity, he'd worked an op with Maggie Sinclair, another now-retired OMEGA agent. The drop-dead-gorgeous Esteban had turned up in Washington some months later, fully intending to follow up on the attraction that had sparked between him and Maggie.

When he found her involved with the man she later married, Luis claimed she'd broken his heart. Maggie knew better, as she laughingly informed Claire when Luis's roving eye descended on the quiet, self-contained psychologist. The colonel's blatant attempts to get Claire into his bed had amused her at first. Then slowly, inevitably, they'd reawakened the sexual appetites that had gone into hibernation after her husband's murder. The man was as skilled a lover as he was persistent.

Esteban now served as Cartoza's ambassador to the U.S. As such, he'd done most of the advance work for President Andrews's now canceled goodwill trip. Claire knew how many hours he'd put into preparing for it, and guessed he would shoulder a heavy dose of responsibility over its abrupt termination.

"Would you wait just a moment, Stacy? I'd like to talk to Ambassador Esteban."

She'd taken only a few steps across the lawn before Luis drew aside with another disembarking passenger. Claire recognized sandy-haired Tom Fogerty, the president's chief of staff. Whipcord lean and intense, he was one of the few Washington insiders retained by President Andrews to facilitate his administration's transition. And by the sound of it, Fogarty was not at all happy with the cancellation of the Central American trip.

"I don't know when we'll reschedule," he told Luis, impatiently shifting his briefcase from hand to hand. "To tell the truth, Mr. Ambassador, Cartoza isn't real high on my list of priorities right now."

"It should be," Luis shot back. "We are the United States's strongest ally in that region."

"Yeah, well, maybe if you'd managed security a little better in your country, we wouldn't have had to cut our visit short."

Luis's jaw locked. Even from several yards away, Claire recognized the warning signs.

"I will tell you one more time, my friend," he said slowly, dangerously. "Stacy Andrews did not eat or drink anything that wasn't first tested by both your people and mine."

"Something caused those nightmares. I still think we'll find they were drug-induced."

"The blood test showed no evidence of hallucinogens. The president informed me of that himself."

"I'm sure he'll want the tests rerun, now that we're back in the States."

The implication was as insulting as Fogerty's sneer.

When Luis narrowed his eyes and gave a low hiss, the politician took a quick step back. Hastily, Claire intervened.

"I'd like to see those test results," she said with cool authority. "I'll obtain the necessary privacy release. If you would, Mr. Fogerty, please ask the president's physician to fax them to my office. Here's my card."

"Right." Keeping a wary eye on Luis, Fogerty pocketed the business card she retrieved from her purse. "And I'll need to know your assessment of Stacy's condition."

"I'm sorry, that's privileged information."

"Not when your patient is the daughter of the president."

"She's not my patient. We're merely going to chat." Claire's normally soft voice was laced with steel. "With Stacy's permission, I may tell her father what we talked about. But he's the *only* one I'll consult or release information to without her specific consent."

Fogerty jerked his head in a quick nod and walked away. Luis followed his progress with narrowed eyes.

"He is an officious bureaucrat, that one. The next time he insults me or my country, he will find himself eating his teeth for breakfast."

For all Claire's training and skill at handling people, she'd yet to learn how best to deal with Luis when something roused his fierce, untempered masculinity. His surge of testosterone at moments like this reflected his passion and his proud Latin heritage.

On a deep instinctive level, she appreciated his tough machismo. He was a man anyone could rely on in a tight situation. She should know. She'd done exactly that several times during the missions they'd worked together.

On a more civilized level, she wanted to calm and soothe and direct his uncompromising maleness into somewhat less combative channels. The eternal female response, when dealing with someone like Luis, she acknowledged with a wry inner smile.

"Can you come for dinner?" she asked quietly. "I'd like your take on what happened."

His expression altered. The heat didn't leave his dark eyes and the testosterone was still zinging through the air, but this time both were directed at her.

"Of course, *mi querida*. I'll bring the wine. Seven o'clock?"

"Seven's good."

Trailed by her Secret Service detail, Stacy Andrews escorted Claire up a flight of stairs in the Executive Residence. The protective agents remained in the hall outside while the girl ushered Claire into a suite of sunny rooms that overlooked the South Lawn.

The suite blended early American history with the distinctive stamp of a lively teenager. A funky lamp with a leopard-print shade sat atop what looked like a genuine Chippendale tea table. Posters of the

Jonas Brothers decorated one wall, a Frederic Church landscape hung on another. A laptop and iPod player occupied a place of honor on an early American slant-lid desk. D.C. schools let out in mid-May for the summer, so there were no backpacks or textbooks scattered around, but Claire noted with approval plenty of teen magazines and paperbacks.

Growing up the daughter of a popular and gregarious governor had instilled Stacy Andrews with social graces beyond her years. Forcing herself to shed some of her reserve, she played the perfect hostess.

"Please, make yourself comfortable, Dr. Cantwell."

Claire chose the oversize sofa, angled to face a wall-hung plasma TV.

"Would you like something to drink?" Stacy asked politely. "Tea? Coffee? A Diet Coke?"

"A Diet Coke would be great."

A small army of staff catered to the First Family's needs, but the teen kept a private stash of goodies in her suite's minikitchen. She poured two soft drinks into ice-filled glasses, then filled a bowl with cheesy Corn Curls.

"These are my favorite munchies," she confided as she positioned the bowl between them on the sofa. "Dad's, too."

Luckily, she'd provided linen napkins with the snack. Claire nibbled on a few morsels and dusted the orange residue from her fingers before taking a sip of cola. She didn't push the subject foremost on both their minds. Instead, she and Stacy chatted idly about other favorite foods and the latest *High School Musical* movie. The subject of the teen's plans for the summer led to an awkward pause.

"I'm going to camp," she said slowly, twisting a strand of dark brown hair around two fingers. "After camp, I was supposed to accompany Dad on another goodwill tour, this one to Asia. I don't know if he'll want to take me after…after what happened in Cartoza."

"What *did* happen, Stacy?"

"I don't know! I mean, I was having fun. I met lots of kids my own age and went to a village fiesta and got to swim with the dolphins at a marine life preserve. Then I had these…these awful dreams."

"Can you describe them for me?"

"There were people. Lots of people dressed in kind of weird clothes."

"Weird how?"

"Old-fashioned, I guess you could call it. And real plain, like they were farmers or something. Some of the women had kerchiefs on their heads. At first they were just standing there, staring at me. Then they… Then they…"

She twisted the strand of hair into a tight spiral. Her breathing sped up. Carefully, Claire watched these visible signs of distress.

"They started crowding closer and closer," Stacy said in a small, scared voice, "until I was surrounded."

She swallowed. Her eyes took on a haunted look that accented the dark shadows under them.

"Then their faces start falling off," she whispered, pushing out each ragged syllable. "The flesh melted away, until they were just skulls with empty eyes. All of them. Just skeletons. Surrounding me. Reaching for me. Like… Like I was going to die and they wanted to drag me into the grave with them!"

She ended on a note of rising panic. Claire anchored her with a calm observation.

"Skeletons quite often appear in dreams, but they don't necessarily symbolize physical death."

Hope replaced the burgeoning fear in the girl's eyes. "They don't?"

"No. In fact, some analysts think they represent life, not death. It could be your subconscious telling you to stop, take a breath, focus on the positive things around you, instead of the negative. Which must be kind of hard to do when you're living in a fishbowl," Claire added shrewdly, "and you see your father's critics on the evening news. It must hurt to hear them question his leadership."

"It does! I hate it when people criticize him. They did it back home, too, when he was governor, but they're so much meaner here."

Claire didn't doubt that. Andrews was playing in the big league now.

"Did you have dreams like this back home?"

"No, never!"

"Tell me what books you've been reading lately. What Web sites you go to, the movies you watch."

With her bright red jacket, jeans and Mary Janes, Stacy Andrews didn't give the appearance of being into Goth or horror, but Claire knew appearances could be very deceptive. Nothing the girl related seemed likely to have implanted the hideous images she'd described, however.

"How about caffeine?" She tapped the frosted glass. "Do you usually have a soft drink before bed?"

"No. Dad says they're not good for me and wants me to limit myself to one or two during the day." Her eyes pleaded with Claire for another explanation. "The dreams really freaked me out, Dr. Cantwell. What else could have caused them?"

"Well, it could have been the stress of the trip,

although threatening dreams such as the ones you've described can result from any number of causes." Lifting a hand, she ticked off a quick list. "Anxiety, illness, loss of a loved one, excessive alcohol consumption, reaction to a drug, sleeping disorders, or even an inherited tendency toward nightmares."

"Dad never mentioned having horrible dreams like this, and he's got a lot more stress than I do."

"How about your mom?" Claire asked gently. "You went through a rough time when you lost her. Do you still miss her?"

"Every day. But…" She worried her lower lip with her teeth for a moment. "It scares me, Dr. Cantwell. Sometimes I have to think real hard to remember what she looked like."

"That's a natural part of healing."

As Claire knew all too well.

"We may not keep their faces or the sound of their voices in our heads, but we keep them here." She laid a palm over her heart, reminded vividly of her own torturous journey. "You don't need to feel guilty for going on with your life, Stacy."

"I don't. At least, I don't think I do."

They talked for a little while longer, and Claire heard nothing that suggested a troubled or deeply disturbed teen.

"Tell you what," she said when they finished. "I'll do some research and get back to you. In the meantime, try to go to bed the same time each night—even on weekends—to reset your sleep cycle. A warm, relaxing bath before you hit the sheets might also help. Also a good thirty-minute workout, if you exercise at least four to five hours before bedtime."

"I can do that."

"I can't promise you won't have these dreams again," Claire cautioned. "If you do, call me and I'll come over. Or you can come to my office. We'll talk you through them and try to understand what they're telling you."

"Thanks, Dr. Cantwell. I'm… I'm not so scared now."

"Good girl. Do you want me to speak to your father about our discussion? I won't, if you'd rather not."

"Sure, you can tell Dad. I'll talk to him, too, and tell him what you said."

Stacy's Secret Service detail remained on duty in the hall while a staff member escorted Claire to the West Wing.

She departed the White House a half hour later, leaving behind a somewhat reassured teenager and a still very worried father. Another staff member drove her back to her office on K Street. Since her very efficient office manager had cleared her schedule after Lightning's call, Claire decided to beat the traffic out of the city and dictate notes of her session with Stacy Andrews at home.

As she drove across the 14th Street Bridge and headed for Alexandria, her thoughts swung between the frightened teenager she'd spent the afternoon with, and the enticing, demanding, occasionally exasperating but always intriguing man she would spend the evening with.

Luis could fill in more details concerning Stacy Andrews's activities while in Cartoza. With a shiver of sensual anticipation, Claire decided he could also make up for the long hours she'd put in at work while he was gone.

She loved her profession. Helping someone through pain or confusion or despair gave her a deep sense of giving back to the world. Her client list kept her extremely busy between the missions she worked for OMEGA. Very often, Claire brought casework home with her, as she had tonight.

She had a large number of friends and acquaintances, as well. Socializing with them and with her tight circle of fellow agents required skilled juggling. Luis had added another dimension to the life Claire had carved out for herself.

And of all the demands on her time and energy, she acknowledged with another ripple of anticipation, Colonel Luis Esteban required the most personal attention.

Chapter 2

Thinking of the evening ahead, Claire turned onto a tree-shaded street in Old Town, Alexandria. After her husband's death, she'd sold their colonial-style home in the suburbs and purchased a three-story townhome. Not only was it closer to her downtown D.C. office, but renovating the town house helped blunt some of her soul-searing grief.

Her home was one of four carved out of an eighteenth-century brick warehouse that had once stored huge barrels of tobacco awaiting shipment from the New World to the Old. Claire had sanded the oak plank floors herself and roamed antique stores on weekends for just the right doorknob and lamp. She'd chosen light, neutral fabrics for the furniture, with jewel-toned throw pillows for the occasional splash of color. Plantation shutters graced the windows throughout the house instead of drapes. In her considered opinion, the result was a perfect blend of new and old, of sunlight and space.

The tranquility of her home welcomed her as she took the stairs from the ground-floor garage to an entry hall lined with oak plank flooring. Once inside, she decided to change before dictating her notes. When working with clients, she wore suits or pantsuits in cool, soothing colors that, theoretically at least, put them at ease. At home she preferred hip-hugging sweats and comfortable T-shirts.

Unless Luis was coming for dinner. Or sex. Or both.

With those tantalizing possibilities ahead, she deposited her briefcase on the foyer table and detoured to the den to click on the built-in stereo system. Humming along with Etta James's smoky rendition of "At Last," she went upstairs.

As always, when she entered her bedroom her glance went first to the crystal-framed photo on the bedside table. It was one of her favorites, snapped during her honeymoon in Hawaii. She and Dave were laughing and splashing through the surf. He looked like he was about to lose his baggy bathing trunks to the undertow. Claire waved to the camera, hoping her new husband didn't moon the woman who'd obligingly offered to take the picture.

"Hard to believe we were ever that young," she murmured with a smile.

Stifling a familiar pang of regret for the years she and Dave had lost, she exchanged her suit for loose-fitting linen slacks with a drawstring waist. She topped those with a colorfully embroidered, off-the-shoulder top she'd picked up during a visit to Cartoza with Luis. He'd taken such delight in showing her his country, she in meeting his friends and family. His parents were dead, but he remained close to his brother, a clutch of sisters, a lively brood of nieces and nephews, and the rather intimidating matriarch of the Esteban clan—a blunt-spoken nonagenarian they all called Tia Maria.

Smiling at the memory of Tia Maria's observation that it was about time Luis chose a woman for her sense instead of her chest size, Claire slid her feet into thong sandals and descended to the kitchen on the main floor of the town house. Cooking for Luis always challenged her admittedly limited culinary skills. Dave had been pretty much a meat-and-potatoes man. Claire's tastes were somewhat more eclectic, but nowhere near Luis's sophisticated palate. Since he'd burst into her life,

he'd introduced her to exotic delicacies she would
never have tried on her own.

Thank goodness she had two swordfish steaks
in the freezer. While they defrosted in the micro-
wave, she prepared a marinade of lemon juice and
white wine. After dousing the steaks, she stuck
them back in the fridge. Sprinkled with slivered
almonds and arranged on a bed of crushed toma-
toes, they would broil in minutes. She assembled
a fresh spinach salad and put that into the fridge,
too. With crusty French bread and a side of wild
rice, the meal should satisfy even Luis's discerning tastes.

Dinner taken care of, Claire went down the hall
to the room she'd had custom-fitted as a combina-
tion library, office and retreat. Bookshelves lined
three walls, high-tech electronic gear the fourth.
Her favorite novels and biographies vied for space
in one section of shelves. Psychology journals and
reference books filled the rest.

She went first to check her faxes. She found
one from the White House—a confidentiality
agreement she needed to sign and return before
they would release Stacy Andrews's medical information, including the results of her most recent
blood test. Claire read the agreement carefully.
Satisfied it conformed to her own professional
standards concerning client privacy, she signed

and dated it. Once she'd faxed it back, she powered up her computer and switched on voice recognition mode.

"Notes from session with Stacy Andrews, fourteen-year-old female, who's experienced two vivid nightmares with debilitating sleep interruption."

She noted the date, time and place of the consultation and described in detail her observations and discussion with the president's daughter. When she finished the dictation, she switched to a powerful search engine that gave her access to a host of databases. Those included the Clinical Psychology Network, with its more than five thousand links, and the American Psychiatric Association's *Diagnostic and Statistical Manual of Mental Disorders.* The link she was most interested in at the moment took her to the National Sleep Foundation.

Claire knew Freud believed dreams expressed unconscious desires, but modern research had tied them to the REM cycle. REM sleep began with a signal from the pons at the base of the brain. The signal was relayed to the cortex, which controlled learning, thinking and organizing information. Although scientists had yet to definitively determine what actually caused dreams, one theory held that the cortex received fragmented signals from the pons and tried to sequence them into thoughts or scenes.

Everyone dreamed. Not everyone remembered their dreams when they woke up. But if the REM cycle was suddenly interrupted or the dreams were vivid or frightening, the sleeper might jerk wake. In that case, they could retain detailed images, as had happened with Stacy Andrews.

Chewing on her lower lip, Claire slid a pad toward her and began making copious notes on the symptoms and treatment for nightmares. That led her to the rare but very dangerous condition known as REM Sleep Behavior Disorder, when individuals got out of bed and began physically acting out their dreams while asleep.

She was still hard at work when the door chimes rang. Startled, she glanced at her watch. Good thing she'd prepared the swordfish before getting lost in her research.

When she opened the door, Luis had to fight to keep his smile lazy. *Madre de Dios!* Did the woman have any idea how seductive she looked?

The last slanting rays of the sun deepened the gold in her pale blond hair and gave her skin a creamy tint. His pulse quickening, Luis followed the clean line of her throat to the slope of her shoulders so enticingly displayed by her blouse.

She excited him in her usual attire of severely

tailored suits and pumps. Cool and serene, she stirred fantasies of slowly stripping away her outer clothing piece by piece until he roused the passion he knew lay underneath.

Like this, though, with her hair falling in a soft cloud to her shoulders and those drawstring pants riding low on her hips, she shoved all thoughts of slow out of his head. His groin tightened, and his greeting took on a husky note.

"Buenas tardes, mi corazón."

"Buenas tardes, Luis."

Her reluctance to use pet names or endearments amused him as much as it had begun to irritate him. He was no overeager young stud. He'd loved passionately once, long ago. Since then, he'd enjoyed mutually satisfying liaisons with a fair number of women. Sophisticated women for the most part, who knew how the game was played and enjoyed playing it. Luis had worked hard to give them as much pleasure as they'd given him. He'd also made sure he parted with each on amicable terms.

But this one, this reserved, self-contained beauty, challenged his masculinity in a way no other woman had. Even in their most intimate moments, she held back a part of herself. Luis hadn't minded at first. He understood and respected her need for privacy in some corners of her life. He was a man with many secrets himself.

Yet what had begun as a familiar, sexual dance had gradually become a test of his will. And hers. One day, he vowed, he'd break through the wall she'd built around her heart since her husband's brutal murder.

"Dinner will be ready shortly," she said as the door closed behind him. "I just have to broil the…"

He snagged her arm, tugged her around.

"First things first."

Depositing the wine he'd brought on the hall table, he thrust his free hand into her hair. The strands threaded between his fingers like air-spun silk.

"I missed you while I was in Cartoza, preparing for President Andrews's visit."

"I missed you, too."

She came into his arms readily and her mouth opened under his. That should have been enough. That, and the way she hooked her arms around his neck and rose up on tiptoe to return the kiss.

Despite her ready kiss—or perhaps because of it—Luis wanted more. Perhaps it was his still-simmering frustration over the president's canceled trip. Perhaps it was the insult from that ass, Fogarty. Whatever it was spurring him sharpened his desire for this woman to a deep, driving need.

He angled his head, found her tongue with his. His hands roamed her back, slid down to cup her bottom and press her against him. He was already hard and aching for her, which made her draw back a little.

"Before dinner?" she asked, with a smile in her eyes.

"Before, during and after," he growled, scooping her into his arms.

His heels rang on the hardwood stairs as he carried her up to the master bedroom. The decor was all Claire—oyster-colored walls, framed Impressionist prints, an inch-thick Turkish carpet in muted jewel tones. Nothing harsh, nothing jarring, everything perfect and in place.

Including the photo in a crystal frame on her bedside table.

Luis wasn't jealous of the husband Claire had loved and lost. On the contrary, that soul-shattering experience had moulded her into the woman she was today. Strong. Self-reliant. Incredibly skilled, both in her profession and the dangerous undercover ops she worked for OMEGA.

Too strong at times. Too self-contained. What ate at him was the knowledge she'd entered this relationship for the same reasons *he'd* entered it. For friendship and intellectual stimulation, as much as sexual satisfaction. The problem was, she seemed content with that.

The atavistic urge to disrupt the tranquil harmony of both the room and the woman in his arms gripped him. A little roughly, he deposited her on the bed and stood over her while he unbuckled his belt and shed his clothing.

Her gaze swept down his chest and flat belly to linger on the erection jutting from the nest of dark hair at his groin. "You *have* missed me," she said with a teasing smile.

Luis was in no mood for teasing. He wanted her wet and hot, as hungry for him as he was for her. At some deeper, primal level, he also wanted her to acknowledge him as a mate as worthy of her as the husband she'd lost.

He took time only to unstrap the ankle holster that was as much a part of him as his suspicious nature and various scars. Naked, he came down beside her. Stretching her arms above her head, he captured her wrists with one hand and yanked at the ties of her slacks with the other.

Her eyes widened, but she obligingly kicked off her sandals and raised her hips. In one swift move, Luis rid her of both slacks and lacy briefs. He tugged up the hem of her blouse, well aware of the fact that she rarely wore a bra at home.

She didn't need one. Her breasts were small and firm and tipped with pink nipples that rose to stiff peaks when he suckled them. Mounding the creamy flesh with his free hand, he bent his head.

Claire dragged in a swift breath. She wasn't sure what lay behind this sudden, Neanderthal approach to sex, but her body responded to it. Her back arched as Luis used his tongue and teeth on her. Pleasure streaked from her breasts to her belly, and her womb clenched in a tight spasm. She could feel the tension building, feel her nerves ignite every place his silky mustache prickled her skin.

His mouth was hot and demanding, his knee insistent, as he wedged it between hers and pried them apart. The psychologist in Claire analyzed the negative cognitions of sexual dominance even as the woman in her responded to his strength and unerring skill.

"Luis," she panted, tugging at her wrists. "Let me touch you. Let me pleasure you."

"Next time, *querida*. This time, I want to pleasure you."

He was good at it. So damned good. His muscled thigh pressed against her sensitive flesh. His mouth claimed hers. When he finally released her wrists and hooked an arm around her waist to position her under him, Claire was wet and ready. And very grateful for the fact they didn't have to resort to condoms.

She'd started birth control again before deciding to yield to Luis's blatant attempts at seduction, but was well aware of his numerous past conquests. They'd been cautious at first, always using the extra protection of a condom. She trusted him enough now, though, to believe him when he swore she was the only woman in his life.

For the moment, anyway. She had no idea how long that would last, but until circumstances changed, she had not the slightest hesitation about welcoming him eagerly into her body.

When he entered her, she could feel each hot, ridged inch. His first thrusts were swift, hard, possessive. She lifted her hips to meet them, and they soon moved together in a rhythm that grew more urgent, more intense, with each grind of their hips.

Her climax began as a swirl of tight, dark sensation. She felt it spiraling up from her belly, tried to contain it. When the sensations exploded in a starburst of exquisite pleasure, she threw her head back, arched her spine and rode the crest.

"Well, we certainly worked up an appetite."

Smiling, Claire sipped her frothy cappuccino and surveyed the remnants of the dinner they'd eaten on the deck. A fat candle flickered inside a glass hurricane lamp. Tiny white lights strung through the vines twisting around the trellised roof added to the glow of a full moon.

She'd pulled on lacy briefs and a celery-colored silk caftan. Luis's scent still clung to her skin, mingling with the fragrant cherry-and-rum aroma of his thin cigarillo and the chocolaty steam rising from the cup she held cradled in both hands.

He sat across from her. He'd raked a hand through his dark hair and left his shirt hanging out, half-buttoned. She liked him this way, Claire mused, as her gaze drifted to the V of bronzed skin dusted with curling black chest air. Relaxed. Comfortable. He was usually so polished and urbane. So much in control. The colonel might have left the military years ago, but the military hadn't left him.

"Tell me what happened in Cartoza," she requested.

"I'm damned if I know." He leaned back in his chair and blew out a cloud of smoke. "I thought everything was going well. President and Señora Diaz welcomed the Andrews to Cartoza with a family luncheon. That afternoon, the two presidents attended the opening session of the Organization of American States. Andrews was welcomed warmly despite the United States' difficulties with some Latin-American countries."

"Like Venezuela," Claire murmured, remembering a particularly nasty op another OMEGA agent had worked on that country's border some months back.

"Like Venezuela," Luis echoed. "While the politicos attended to business, Señora Diaz gave Stacy a tour of the capital. They were accompanied by the fourteen-year-old girl who recently won our national spelling bee. And, of course, a full contingent of both U.S. and Cartozan security forces. I vetted every one of our people myself."

Claire didn't doubt it. As former chief of Cartoza's security forces, Luis would not take the challenges associated with a visiting head of state lightly.

"The first nightmare came well after midnight, close to four a.m. I didn't learn of it until several hours later. I also learned the physician accompanying Andrews's party had administered a sedative and Stacy had slept for the rest of the night."

Frowning, he rolled the thin cigar in his fingers.

"She appeared happy and quite normal the next morning, although you could see the fatigue in her eyes. We altered her schedule so it included only the events we thought she would most enjoy. Stacy and Rosa—the spelling bee champion—splashed in the Dolphin Cove with a group of other youngsters. That afternoon they attended a village fiesta. It was very colorful, crowded and noisy, but I swear to you, Claire, my people tested everything before she ate or drank it. I'm ninety-nine-point-nine percent certain no one slipped her any kind of drug or hallucinogen."

"It certainly seems unlikely, but you and I have been in this business long enough to know anything is possible. So the second nightmare occurred that night, after the fiesta?"

"It did."

His mouth grim, Luis stubbed out his cigarillo in the ashtray Claire kept out on the deck for his use. He never lit up inside and always took care to stand or sit downwind, so as not to expose her to secondhand smoke.

She would have liked him to give the habit up completely, but the casual nature of their relationship didn't give her the right to request that kind of behavioral modification. Unless or until that relationship changed, she actually enjoyed an occasional whiff of the rum-and-cherry smoke.

"Did the White House fax you the results of the blood test they administered after the second nightmare?" he wanted to know.

"I had to sign and send back a confidentiality agreement first. The results may have come in in the past few hours…while I was otherwise engaged."

"Will you inform me if the actual results are different from what I was told?"

"No."

Her calm reply produced only a small shrug. Luis had learned enough about Claire's profession—and about her—during their months together to have expected no other answer. He also knew she would do her best to keep him in the loop, however. Especially with his prickly macho pride and national honor at stake.

"If they *are* different," she assured him, "I'll ask Stacy or her father if I can discuss them with you."

She tapped a nail against her cappuccino cup. A item from the notes she'd dictated tugged at her thoughts.

"Do you know what the women at the fiesta were wearing? The village women?"

The question surprised him. "Their best garments, I would guess. As you know well, the women of my county love bright colors. They would have worn ruffled skirts in red and turquoise and green. Embroidered blouses trimmed with colorful ribbons. That sort of thing."

"What about on their heads?"

"The girls usually wear garlands of flowers, the older women lace mantillas."

"Flowers and lace, not kerchiefs?"

"Some may have covered their hair with cloth mantles. Why do you ask this?"

"It was just something Stacy said. A fragment of the dream she remembered."

Luis's gaze sharpened. "You think a woman wearing a head covering may have frightened her and caused her to have these nightmares?"

"I haven't formulated any viable theories as to their root cause yet. I had just dictated my notes and begun my research when you arrived."

"Nevertheless, I'll query the captain who commanded her escort and have him review the footage from the festival. If Stacy spoke to or came in contact with a woman wearing a mantle, it should be on the surveillance videos."

Being able to take some action, any action, seemed to reenergize him.

"Are you done with your cappuccino, my heart? If so, I'll carry the dishes into the kitchen."

"I'm finished."

When she rose to help gather the plates, he nudged her aside.

"You cooked, I'll clean. Go, finish this research I interrupted. Then *we* will finish what we began earlier."

Luis made sure their second session was as slow and sweet as the first was fierce. He would have made it last until dawn, if Claire hadn't finally driven him over the edge.

His chest heaving, he sprawled bonelessly amid the tangled sheets until the world stopped spinning. She lay with her head nested on his shoulder, her hair spilling across his chest and the musky scent of their lovemaking teasing his nostrils. Idly, he played with strands of her hair as the thoughts that had tugged at him when she'd opened the door to him earlier once again played through his mind.

Why couldn't he seem to get enough of this slender, maddeningly independent woman? How was it that she satisfied his every carnal desire, yet left him wanting more?

God knows he was a self-professed connoisseur of women. Some he'd admired for their beauty, some for their intelligence or talent or sparkling personalities. But this one… This one stirred urges that edged dangerously close to that vague, ill-defined emotion the poets labeled love.

Luis had teetered on the brink of that emotion only once before. The affair had flamed hot and ended in a murderous cross fire. Since then, he'd limited himself to mutually satisfying liaisons with no commitments on either side. Yet lying here, stroking Claire's hair, breathing in her scent…

"Shall I stay the night, *querida?*"

"What time is it?" she murmured sleepily.

He flicked a look at the bedside clock. His glance

lingered on the crystal frame for a second before he replied.

"Almost two."

"Mmm." She buried her nose in the warm skin of his neck. "Too late for you to drive back into the city and rouse the embassy staff. Stay the night."

"What if I stay longer?" He gave her hair another slow stroke. "Or don't leave at all?"

The question bought her blinking awake, as he'd known it would. Pushing upright, she propped herself on an elbow. Her hair fell across her forehead. When she hooked the loose strand behind her ear, he saw her face clearly in the moonlight streaming through the top half of the plantation shutters. Saw, too, the question in her eyes.

"We agreed up front that we both need our space, Luis. We discussed boundaries."

"Perhaps it's time to renegotiate those boundaries."

"Why?"

"I want more of you, Claire."

"You have all I'm prepared to give right now," she said quietly. "All I *can* give."

He was formulating his response to that when the phone beside the bed shrilled. Rolling over, she lifted the receiver.

"Dr. Cantwell."

A few clicks sounded, then a disembodied voice

announced that the line was secure. That was followed by a terse request that came through clearly enough for Luis to overhear.

"This is Tom Fogerty, Dr. Cantwell. Can you come to the Executive Residence right away?"

"Of course. Is it Stacy?"

"Yes. She's had another episode. She's sobbing hysterically and asking for you."

Chapter 3

When an aide escorted Claire into the Executive Residence, an assortment of staff members and Secret Service agents hovered in the hall outside Stacy's bedroom.

Sandy-haired Tom Fogarty was among them looking tense, hastily dressed in jeans and a knit shirt with one edge of the collar turned under. He greeted Claire with undisguised relief, then opened the door to the same suite she'd visited the day before and stuck his head in.

"Dr. Cantwell's here, sir."

"Ask her to come in."

Fogarty closed the door behind Claire, leaving

her alone with the president and his daughter. They sat huddled side by side on the sofa in the sitting room. Every lamp was lit in that room and the room beyond. Claire caught a glimpse of the bed with its covers thrown off and onto the floor, as if the occupant had struggled violently with them.

The president sat beside his daughter with an arm around her shoulders. One glance told Claire that Stacy had yet to recover from her terrifying dream. Above her pink cotton sleep shirt, her face was splotchy and her eyes red from crying.

The president didn't look much better. Claire saw no trace of his trademark boyish charm. Belted into a navy robe with the presidential seal embroidered on the pocket, he greeted her calmly, but the deep crease in his brow showed he was a very worried father.

"Thanks for coming, Dr. Cantwell. Sorry to drag you out in the middle of the night."

"It's not a problem, Mr. President. Hi, Stacy." Sympathy for the girl softened her voice. "This must have been a bad one."

The teen shuddered. "It was awful."

"Do you feel up to telling me about it? It's difficult, I know, but I'd like to hear whatever details you can remember before your subconscious suppresses them."

"Will it?" she asked with a desperate need for reassurance. "Make me forget all this, I mean?"

"That's normally what happens."

At the president's invitation, Claire took the chair angled toward the sofa.

"Would you like coffee?" he asked. "That's a fresh carafe. They just brought it up a few minutes ago."

"I'm fine for now, thanks."

"Okay." He glanced from Claire to his hunch-shouldered daughter. "Do you want me to leave while you talk to Dr. Cantwell, Stace? I'll wait outside in the hall. You can call me when you're done."

"No." She clutched at the lapel of his robe. "Stay, Daddy. Please."

"Sure. If that's okay with Dr. Cantwell?"

"Certainly. I'd like to record this session so I won't be distracted by taking notes or have to try to remember everything later. Is that all right with you, Stacy?"

"I guess so."

Claire extracted a microrecorder from her purse and clicked it on. After noting the time, date, location and name of the client, she slipped the recorder into the pocket of her pantsuit.

"Out of sight, out of mind," she told the other two with a smile. "Okay, Stacy. Tell me whatever you can remember from your dream."

In a choked whisper, the teen described a dream sequence very similar to the one she'd related to Claire earlier that day. Crowds of people surrounding around her, reaching for her. Women in aprons and kerchiefs. One man, she thought, was holding some kind of wooden pitchfork. Bit by bit, their flesh began to melt away. Their eyes became empty sockets. Until they were just rank upon rank of skulls, skeletons, disjointed bones.

"There was something else." Forehead furrowed, she tried to remember. "Some kind of vault or crypt or something."

Her hand crept across the sofa cushion to clutch her father. White-knuckled, she continued in a ragged whisper.

"I remember stepping down some stairs. I know I felt cold. Icy cold. I think I heard music or chanting. There were more bones. So many bones. Then I could sense…"

She gulped, breathing hard. Claire ached at the fear reflected in the girl's eyes.

"I could sense… I could feel my own skin sagging and starting to fall off. I screamed for help. But they just looked at me, Dr. Cantwell! All those skulls, all those skeletons. They just looked at me with their dead, empty eyes. Does it mean I'm going to die?" she asked on a note of sheer panic.

"Absolutely not. We talked about this yesterday,

remember? Dreams aren't harbingers of the future. They're an amalgam of your subconscious, fractured thoughts. Our task now is to determine what's implanting those thoughts."

She shifted her attention to the president.

"I told Stacy yesterday that threatening dreams like this one could stem from a number of causes. Stress might be a major factor, as could illness, sleeping disorders, drug reactions or the loss of a loved one."

The crease between president's brow deepened. Out of that list, the loss of a loved one had to have hit him as hard as it had his daughter. With a tug of sympathetic understanding, Claire continued calmly.

"I think we should rule out possible physical factors first. I'd like to talk to your doctor and set up a complete physical for Stacy. I'd also like you to consider allowing me to schedule her for a sleep study."

"What does that involve?"

"The studies generally include a polysomnogram, which records a number of body functions while the subject is sleeping. Like brain activity, eye movement, heart rate and carbon dioxide blood levels. Also, we'll conduct a Multiple Sleep Latency Test. That measures how long it takes the subject to fall asleep."

"Where would these tests be conducted?" Stacy wanted to know.

"In a hospital sleep lab. Georgetown University Hospital has an excellent one. So does the University of Maryland Medical Center. I'm sure Bethesda does, too, although I'm not as familiar with it as the other two."

The president and his daughter exchanged glances. "What do you think, Stace?"

"I trust Dr. Cantwell. I'm okay with whatever she suggests."

"Good." Slipping a hand into her pocket, Claire clicked off the recorder. "I'll get with your physician and set the tests up. Don't worry, Stacy. Between us, we'll figure what's causing these dreams."

"I hope so! I'm supposed to leave for camp next month."

To redirect the teen's thoughts from the nightmares, Claire asked her about the camp's activities. Stacy perked up when describing the summer camp for disabled children, where she'd served as a counselor last year and hoped to again this year.

They chatted until she ran out of steam and her lids began to droop. When she put up a hand to cover a wide yawn, Claire knew it was time to end the session.

"Sleepy, Stacy?"

"Yes."

"You hit the sack," her father instructed. "I'll step outside for a moment to talk to Dr. Cantwell, then I'll bunk down here on the sofa for the rest of the night."

"You don't have to do that, Dad!"

"I don't *have* to, but I want to."

"Okay. Thanks, Dr. Cantwell."

"You're welcome. We'll talk again when I have the tests set up."

"I want them done right away," the president told Claire when they went into the hall and he'd waved back the handful of staff so they could speak privately. "Today, if possible."

"I'll make the calls this morning."

"She's the most important person in my life, Dr. Cantwell." His Adam's apple worked. "Whatever it takes, whatever I have to do, I'll do it to give her a normal, happy childhood. Even if it means resigning."

"I'm confident it won't come to that."

"I hope not!" He thrust a hand through his hair. "But the stress of this job is unimaginable. Far more than I'd anticipated, even with my years as a governor. And the complete lack of privacy. You're surrounded, every minute of the day. If that's what's giving Stacy these nightmares…" His voice took on a gruff edge. "If that's what's making her so scared…"

"We don't know that's the root cause. There are many other possibilities. Including," she added, "an inherited tendency. May I ask, sir, do you dream?"

"If I do, I don't remember the details after waking up."

"What about Stacy's mom? Did she have nightmares?"

"Occasionally, now that I think about it." His forehead furrowed. "But Teo's dreams were never like this."

"Teo?"

Like the rest of America, Claire had read numerous articles during the long campaign that touched on John Andrews's deceased wife. None of those articles had referred to her by anything other than Anne Elizabeth Andrews.

"Teodora was her confirmation name," the president explained. "She got it from her grandfather on her mother's side."

A brief smile flitted across his face, easing the lines of stress. For a moment he looked like the boyishly handsome president who'd taken office just months ago.

"Teodore Cernak was one of the toughest old coots I've ever met," he told Claire. "He was just sixteen when the Nazis invaded Czechoslovakia in '38. They conscripted him into the navy, but he deserted a year later and stowed away in the hold of a cargo ship. He snuck into this country with less than five dollars in his pocket. Twenty years later, the man owned and operated nineteen dry-cleaning shops and still cussed like a sailor."

"He must have passed some of that toughness to Stacy. She's a remarkable young woman, Mr. President. Together, we'll get her through this rough patch."

Dawn streaked the ink-black sky when Claire drove down her quiet Alexandria street. As she neared her town house she saw the sleek sports car Luis drove when not on official embassy duties still parked at the curb.

Deep in thought, she hit the garage remote. In the rush to get to the White House, Luis's suggestion that it might be time to renegotiate their agreed-upon boundaries had slipped to the back of her mind. She hadn't had time to reflect on it, much less formulate a response.

She wasn't up to tackling that kind of discussion now, however. Their two deliciously exhausting sessions between the sheets and the hours she'd spent at 1600 Pennsylvania Avenue had her running on reserve.

Luis, thank goodness, recognized that immediately. He was in the kitchen, settled comfortably at the island counter with the early edition of the *Washington Post* and a mug of coffee. He'd showered, Claire saw from the dampness glistening in his black hair. And shaved. The prickly stubble that scraped her inner thighs last night was gone.

"How is Stacy?" he asked.

"Shaken."

That's all Claire would say, despite his very direct involvement in the situation. He understood and accepted the concise reply with a nod.

"I hope you can help her."

"I'm certainly going to try."

When she shrugged off her shoulder bag and dropped it on the counter, he skimmed a discerning eye over her face.

"You look exhausted."

"I am."

"Shall I make you breakfast? Eggs scrambled with sausage and salsa?"

"As tempting as that sounds, I'll pass. What I need right now is a shower, followed by a power nap. Then I have to hit the phones."

"I understand."

When he eased off the stool and crossed the room, his scent enveloped her. Claire succumbed to a moment of weakness. Sliding her arms around his waist, she leaned against his chest.

"God, you smell good."

"Do you think so?" One jet-black eyebrow arched. "My staff will no doubt smirk when I arrive home smelling of your perfumed soap. I must bring my own next time. And a shaving kit to leave here." He scraped a palm across his chin. "Your plastic razor does not do the job on my bristles."

"Boundaries," she murmured. "We'll talk about them later. When we're not so tired."

He curled a knuckle under her chin and tipped her face to his. "Yes, *querida*. We will."

His mouth brushed hers. The kiss was whisper light, yet made Claire rethink her immediate priorities.

"Now go," he instructed, "take your nap. I'll let myself out."

Why was she resisting?

Her face raised to the pulsing shower stream, Claire let the water needle into her skin.

Why not take her relationship with Luis to the next level? He was intelligent, charming and a fascinating companion. Not to mention an incredibly skilled lover. Claire hadn't enjoyed such fantastic sex since…since…

Her thoughts stumbled. It took an effort of will to articulate the emotion pinging at her. Guilt, tinged with a nagging sense of disloyalty.

The truth was, she'd *never* experienced such incredible sex. Dave had been as thoughtful and considerate and fun in bed as he was out of it. Yet, after those first heady years of courtship and marriage, they'd settled into what Claire now recognized as a comfortable sexual routine.

She leaned against the wet tiles and tried to imagine Luis Esteban settling into *any* kind of a routine, comfortable or otherwise. The man had held a host of military, governmental and diplomatic positions, each one more responsible than the last. He moved with the same confidence among kings and presidents as he had with the troops he'd once commanded. What's more, he was at his lethal best in tight, dangerous situations. Claire could personally attest to that.

A closer relationship would require significant compromise on her part. And a considerable attitude adjustment on his. The colonel retained just enough chauvinism under that handsome, sophisticated exterior to make Claire wary. The beast was subdued, but not tamed.

Sighing, she pushed the Luis question aside for later reflection and lathered up. Mere moments later, she set the internal alarm clock she'd relied on more than once in the field and fell facedown into the pillows.

Her inner alarm didn't fail her. She woke a little more than an hour later feeling invigorated. It was still too early to make calls, so she brewed a fresh pot of coffee and breakfasted on a toasted bagel.

She took the second cup to her office. The bits Stacy had related about the clothing of the people in the nightmares kept nagging at her. Kerchiefs and aprons? A wooden pitchfork? That didn't sound like Cartoza. Luis's country was one of the more progressive and economically advanced in Central America.

It did, however, sound like clothing and utensils used by farmers and country dwellers seventy-five or eighty years ago. About the time Stacy's great-grandfather would have stowed away on a ship bound for the States.

Following a hunch, Claire powered up her laptop to continue the research Luis had interrupted last night. Only, this time she focused on case studies relating to nightmares experienced by individuals of Slavic descent.

She found several. One examined the violent dreams of people who'd survived Stalin's brutal regime. Another looked at dream differentiation between western, eastern and southern Slavs. The third's title was in a foreign language, but the English translation beneath snagged Claire's instant interest: *A Theological Treatise on Skeletal Apparitions Recurring in Dreams of the People in Central Bohemia.*

The study was more than six decades old and had been authored by a Father Josef Tuma. Intrigued, Claire clicked back to Google to pinpoint Bohemia's location. She *thought* it had been part of the old Hapsburg empire, broken up after Germany lost WWI. She also knew the word Bohemian referred to the unconventional, Gypsy-like lifestyle adopted by artists, writers and actors during the nineteenth century. Beyond that, she had no clue.

A quick online search revealed the Eastern European region known as Bohemia had been variously populated or controlled by Celts, Slavs, Romans, Magyars, Hussites, Hungarians, Germans, Czechoslovakians and Soviets. In 1993, Bohemia became part of the newly established Czech Republic.

Claire's pulse kicked up. She had no proof as yet that Stacy's nightmares stemmed from an inherited tendency. But it certainly wouldn't hurt to ask the president exactly what part of the country formerly known as Czechoslovakia his wife's grandfather had emigrated from.

Her excitement turned to disappointment when she clicked on the link to Father Tuma's study and discovered the Web page no longer existed. Frowning, she picked up the phone. A three-digit code connected her directly to

OMEGA's control center and identified her immediately to the agent on duty.

"Hey, Cyrene. What's up?"

Her code name was now as familiar to her as the second skin she slid into during her missions for OMEGA. She'd chosen it when she first started with the agency years ago. She certainly couldn't claim the physical strength of the mythical Cyrene, who'd wrestled the lion that attacked her father's sheep, and in the process, caught Apollo's admiring, amorous eye. But Claire had discovered an inner core of strength she hadn't known she possessed after Dave's brutal murder.

"Hi, Rigger," she replied. "I need to get my hands on a document I found on the Internet. When I click on its link, though, I get a message indicating the page no longer exists."

"E-mail me the link. I'll have our folks work it."

"The document is written in Czech."

That didn't faze Joe Devlin, code name Rigger. Oklahoma born and bred, he took his code name from the rigs he'd worked on prior to joining OMEGA. Like those rigs, he was as tough as steel beneath his easygoing exterior.

"No problem," he said in his lazy drawl. "If we can retrieve the document, I'll send it to the Czech embassy and get it translated."

"Thanks. I also need to give Lightning an update on the situation with the president's daughter. Would you ask him to contact me when he comes in?"

"He's already hard at it downstairs. Hang on, I'll patch you through to his office."

Her boss's early arrival shouldn't have surprised Claire. A former operative himself, Nick Jensen took his responsibilities as OMEGA's director seriously.

"I have Cyrene on the line," Rigger informed him. "She has an update for you. Go ahead, Cyrene."

Claire provided a succinct account of her middle-of-the-night call and second session with Stacy Andrews. She also relayed the president's deep-seated concern—and his blunt declaration that he'd resign his office if necessary to protect his child.

Lightning muttered an oath. "Be a shame to lose the first president in a long time who's not afraid to take on powerful lobbies and entrenched congressional interests. Stay on this, Cyrene. Whatever assets or support you need, you've got."

Claire understood that without being told. The ramifications of President Andrews's resignation so soon into his term would impact every facet of government operations.

"Keep me posted," her boss instructed.

"I will."

* * *

The next three days whizzed by in a frenzy of activity.

The White House physician orchestrated a complete physical workup on Stacy. Between those tests, Claire administered a series of psychological measurements.

Miraculously, Tom Fogarty somehow managed to keep those activities off the media's radar. Claire could only imagine Stacy's embarrassment if word leaked about her nightmares and she saw them splashed across the headlines, or discussed ad nauseam by the talking heads on TV news shows.

To the profound relief of both the president and his daughter, every physical and psychological test indicated she was a happy, well-balanced, healthy teen. The results of the sleep study conducted at Georgetown University Hospital were similarly reassuring.

Measurement of Stacy's rapid eye movement during sleep fell well within the normal range. Her AHI—Apnea-Hypopnea Index—indicated a very low frequency per hour of respiratory events. That obviated Claire's worry the girl might routinely stop breathing for short periods during sleep, thus reducing the oxygen supply to the brain and possibly causing the fractured thoughts that wove into bad dreams.

It may have been the test results, or simply the reassurance that her nightmares didn't presage imminent death. Whatever the reason, Stacy slept undisturbed for several nights in a row. Everyone concerned was just beginning to breathe easy when she woke screaming and drenched in sweat again.

Claire spent another dawn at the White House, talking the girl down from her terror. Afterward, she met with the president and Tom Fogarty in the Oval Office. The vice president sat in on this meeting as well.

Silver-haired and shrewd, the VP had served six terms in the Senate and one as Secretary of Defense. He'd brought the Washington insider experience to the ticket that John Jefferson Andrews lacked. If the rumor mill was right, he was now drawing extensively on that experience, to soothe the feathers Andrews ruffled right and left with his clean-sweep policies.

Daniel Molineaux's presence reinforced the gravity of the situation. Claire knew the vice president wouldn't be there if Andrews hadn't tipped him off to the possibility he might resign.

"I'm beginning to suspect these nightmares may be genetic," she told the three men. "We've ruled out everything else. Do you know the region your wife's grandfather emigrated from?" she asked the president.

"I'm not sure of the exact region." Wearily, the president scrubbed a hand over the back of his neck. "It was somewhere in what used to be Czechoslovakia. Bohemia, I think. Why?"

Claire's pulse tripped. Maybe, just maybe, she'd stumbled on a possible link.

"I found a brief synopsis of a treatise written by a priest in Bohemia more than a half century ago. The study describes nightmares startlingly similar to the ones Stacy has experienced. I've tried to track down a copy, hoping it would help me pinpoint the root cause of Stacy's dreams, but it's proved hard to come by."

To her disappointment, the computer wizards at OMEGA hadn't been able to trace the broken link. Yet. OMEGA's guru of all things electronic—who also happened to be Lightning's wife, Mackenzie—had taken that one on as a personal challenge.

Nor had the Czech embassy been able to locate a copy. They had, however, located its author. Father Josef Tuma was now Cardinal Tuma, and served as the Archbishop of Prague. Claire had tried to contact him, but the cardinal was in his late eighties and increasingly frail. According to his assistant, his eminence's bad days now outnumbered the good, and he would soon retire and retreat from public life.

"Do you need additional resources to work the problem?" the president asked tersely.

"I'll advise if I do. In the meantime…"

She had little additional advice to offer, besides what she'd given Stacy during their first session. An exercise session at least five hours before bed, soothing baths, relaxing music on the iPod she was never without, and as normal a routine as possible.

The vice president walked Claire to the security checkpoint. Daniel Molineaux had conducted a hard-fought primary campaign against John Andrews. In the way of politics, the once-bitter rivals had joined forces after the primary. Their combined ticket of youthful charisma and decades of experience had proved irresistible to voters. As a result, the longtime Washington insider many thought had a lock on the office of the president now served as an outsider determined to shake things up.

Molineaux had to find his new role as arbiter between John Andrews and the Washington establishment a challenge, yet he seemed to be carrying it off. Not that Claire was privy to the closed-door sessions and private deals that formed the stuff of life in D.C. Still, the general impression was that the vice president was doing his best to support a president whose views he'd vigorously opposed during the primary.

That could all change now, though, depending on what happened with Stacy Andrews. The man who'd fought so hard to win the Oval Office was once again within striking distance. The prospect put a deep crease between his thick, snowy brows.

"How confident are you that you'll find the root cause of Stacy's nightmares, Dr. Cantwell?"

She was more hopeful than confident at this point.

"I'll keep working the problem until I find some way to help her."

Nodding, he echoed the president's grim assurances. "All the assets of the White House are at your disposal. Just ask, and we'll supply whatever you need."

"I will," she promised.

Another case claimed Claire's attention for most of the following day.

A battered wife and mother she'd counseled for several years took a brutal beating from her ex-cop husband. The hospital contacted Claire. She spent hours with the distraught, utterly despairing woman. More hours arranging shelter for her and her children.

At the wife's urgent request, she accompanied the shattered family to the shelter and saw them settled before meeting Luis for a late dinner at their favorite Asian restaurant in Old Town. He listened gravely while she related some of the details of her troubling day. Only later, as they left the restaurant, did she bring up the other case weighing heavily on her mind.

"I may have to fly to Prague."

Arm in arm, they strolled through the spring night. The restaurant was only a few blocks from Claire's condo. Too close to drive, even if the night hadn't been so warm and balmy. Besides, she knew Luis would take advantage of the open air to light up. The tip of his thin cigar glowed in the dusk as he gave her a questioning glance.

"Prague? Why?"

"I've been trying to track down an old document that describes dreams such as the ones Stacy's been having. We haven't found the document itself, but we have located the priest who wrote it. He's now a cardinal and holds the title of Archbishop of Prague, although age and ill health may dictate his retirement from that post any day."

"Can you not just call or e-mail him to request a copy?"

"I tried that. Unfortunately, he doesn't have a copy in his possession. The priest who serves as his executive assistant indicated his eminence would be willing to speak with me about it—if I caught him on one of his good days."

A sliver of moon drifted through the trees lining

the street. Their footsteps echoed on the pavement. Flicking an ash from the tip of his pencil-thin cigar, Luis took Claire's arm to guide her over a patch of cobblestones laid in the eighteenth century.

They'd just reached the stairs leading up to Claire's front door when a figure dressed in black lunged out of the shadows.

Chapter 4

Claire's years as a field operative had honed her reflexes to a razor's edge. Luis's were every bit as quick, but their attacker had the advantage of surprise. Before either of them could do more than twist toward the source of the threat, he had a fist in Claire's hair and a knife to her jugular.

"Don't do it!" he snarled at Luis. "I'll cut her throat!"

Luis caught himself in mid-lunge. By sheer force of will, he aborted the counterassault.

All his training and years of experience coalesced into this moment, this instant. In the space of a single heartbeat, he assessed the situation.

It didn't take longer than that instant to know the subcompact Glock strapped to his ankle was useless. Every defense expert in the world emphasized that a knife to the throat was the most dangerous and difficult attack to defeat. Conventional wisdom said to go along with the attacker, placate him, do nothing to provoke him into slashing his blade from right to left.

Luis had no choice but to follow that route. One flick of the mugger's wrist, one misstep on Luis's part, and Claire would bleed to death before his eyes.

"What do you want?" he bit out, forcing himself to catalog the few features visible through the mugger's black ski mask.

"What do think I want? Empty your pockets. Put everything in your woman's purse. Throw it to him, bitch. Now!"

With her head tilted back at an awkward angle, Claire shrugged off her shoulder bag and made a clumsy toss. Luis caught it and dropped his billfold inside.

"That gold watch, too."

His Rolex joined his wallet.

"Stretch out your arm and pass the purse back to your woman."

Her throat exposed to the gleaming blade, Claire retrieved the shoulder bag.

This was the decision point. She knew it. Luis knew it. Their eyes locked in an instant of raw communication. If all the mugger intended was robbery, he'd grab the purse, shove Claire at Luis and take off. Or try to.

If he didn't…

Claire's eyes telegraphed an unmistakable signal. She'd planned her move. The knowledge stopped Luis's heart dead in his chest.

For another half second, the issue hung in the balance. Then the mugger bent his head and whispered something in her ear.

That was the moment, the slight distraction, Claire had been waiting for. In a move so swift it caught her attacker by complete surprise, she thrust her chin to the side and wedged it between her throat and the hand holding the knife. In the same instant, she shot her fist through the narrow angle opened by the wedge. The thrust widened the opening and gave her just enough space to duck under his arm.

Her elbow locked in his, she twisted down, around and up again. Speed and momentum gave her the leverage to yank him with her, bending him almost double in the process.

Luis moved with equal speed. In one swift chop, he brought the edge of his hand slicing down. He'd delivered the same blow countless times before.

This time, the target turned his head at precisely the wrong instant.

Instead of slamming into the back of his neck, the lethal karate chop crushed his windpipe. The mugger gave a low, strangled gurgle and crumpled. Twitching and gagging, he clawed at his throat.

Claire tried to aid him. Cursing, she dropped to her knees and rolled him over, but there was nothing she could do for him. Even before he flopped onto his back, his eyes had rolled up in his head and his hands had dropped to his side.

"He's dead," she confirmed after searching for a pulse.

She was her cool, controlled self. Luis's adrenaline still pumped like a fire hose. He didn't feel a shred of remorse or guilt. Any thug who held a knife to a woman's throat deserved what he got. Particularly *his* woman's throat.

Hunkering down, he pulled off the ski mask. He expected to find a young street tough under the knit mask, but the face that stared blankly up at the night sky belonged to a man in his mid to late thirties.

Frowning, Luis draped a forearm across his knee. The smooth-shaven face and close-cropped hair didn't fit the typical thug. Nor did the clothes. Pleated black slacks, black turtleneck, black gloves. This was no mugger taking a target of opportunity. This was a planned hit.

When Luis pushed to his feet, Claire keyed 911 on her cell phone. She relayed her name, location and the nature of the emergency. She also confirmed she and her companion were unharmed, but their attacker was dead.

"What did this one whisper to you?" Luis asked when she hung up.

She hooked a loose strand behind her ear, her brow knitting. "He said this time was a warning. That'd I'd better back off."

"Back off? From what?"

"I didn't wait to hear. I knew I had to take advantage of that instant of distraction to counter his attack."

"Which was beyond foolish, Claire!"

The emotions Luis had held so savagely in check during the attack broke free.

"If this one came to issue a warning, he did not intend to kill you! You should have waited, let him make his next move. You must know how dangerous that countermove was."

"Yes," she replied with a lift of one delicately arched brow, "I do."

"Madre de dios!"

Luis had to remind himself she was a trained agent. He'd witnessed her skills in the field. But to see that blade beneath her chin… To know one flick of the wrist, one slice… He never wanted to feel such terror again.

The distant wail of sirens broke into his chaotic thoughts. Within moments, he and Claire were involved in the complicated business of death.

The first responders were uniformed police officers. They were followed in short order by a crime scene unit, two homicide detectives and representatives from the county medical examiner's office.

Luis's diplomatic status added another layer to the process. The responding officers barely suppressed a groan at the prospect of the paperwork connected to an incident involving a credentialed ambassador. The evidence pointed so clearly to self-defense, however, that the homicide detectives who assessed the scene merely took his statement and said they'd get in touch with him if they needed further information. What interested them more was the deceased's whispered warning to Claire and the fact that he carried no ID of any kind.

"The guy was a pro," the lead detective mused as the body was loaded into the meat wagon. "Sounds like robbery was a secondary motive for the attack. You say he didn't indicate what he wanted you to back away from, Dr. Cantwell?"

"No, he didn't."

"You working a case or a client that might have someone worried enough to hire a pro to come after you?"

"I have more than thirty clients in varying stages of therapy. Twice that number who come for periodic follow-up. A good number are dealing with severely dysfunctional domestic or work situations."

Like the case she'd worked just today, she related grimly. The husband who put his wife in the hospital was an ex-cop.

"We'll check him out," Detective Waterman promised. "And anyone else in your case files you think might have reason to warn you off. In the meantime, we'll see if the coroner can ID this character."

It was almost midnight by the time the crime scene unit wrapped up and the detectives finished interviewing the neighbors who'd emerged from adjoining town houses in response to the sirens and lights. Most were shocked by such a violent crime right on their doorsteps, and no one had seen or heard anything prior to the attack.

Claire had used the interval to relay a report of the incident to OMEGA control and assure them both she and Luis were unharmed. She was beginning to feel a delayed response to the vicious attack, though, when she and Luis finally entered the serene, undisturbed sanctuary of her home.

She didn't communicate her sudden flutter of nerves to Luis. She didn't have to. He'd been in enough dangerous situations to anticipate the after-effect. One glance at her face in the bright lights of her foyer produced a terse announcement.

"I will stay tonight."

He didn't frame it as a request. Normally, a flat dictum like that would have triggered a cool response. Tonight, Claire readily acquiesced.

"I can't think of any more effective post-traumatic therapy for either of us than to proceed upstairs immediately and savor the hot, rich sweetness of life."

Amusement flickered in his dark eyes. "That, *mi corazón,* is the best excuse for taking you to bed I've heard yet."

They savored the sweetness twice.

Once with Claire straddling Luis's hips and her palms planted on the hard, muscled planes of his chest. And again the next morning, when sunbeams sifted through the plantation shutters and bathed the bedroom in soft light. Boneless and satiated, Claire lolled amid the tangled sheets while Luis showered.

Although neither of them had so much as mentioned boundaries, she knew in her heart they'd stretched them last night. Her hair rustled on the pillow as she turned her head.

Her gaze lingered on the photo beside the bed for long moments. They'd been so young, she and Dave. So happy. A familiar ache started just under her ribs.

Claire stared at the photo for several more moments before tossing aside the top sheet. She took Luis's shirt off the bedpost and slid her arms into the fine-spun cotton. The shirttails brushed her naked thighs as she lifted the heavy crystal fame.

She would always have the memories. Nothing could erase them or the love she and Dave had shared. But it wasn't fair to Luis to keep a reminder of that love here, where it was the first thing he saw when he rolled out of her bed. Not if he and Claire were going to take their relationship to the next level.

She thought about what that level should entail as she went downstairs to make coffee. Barefoot and still wearing only Luis's shirt, she carried two mugs back upstairs. She'd worked out a set of satisfactory parameters in her mind by the time Luis emerged from the shower.

He had a towel wrapped low on his hips and used another to dry his hair. Ruefully, Claire wondered when the hell she'd regressed to the point that the mere sight of a bronzed, muscled torso and a killer smile could get her wet.

"I've been thinking," she said, as she handed him one of the mugs. "No reason for your whiskers to keep dulling my razor. Why don't you bring a shaving kit to leave here." She skimmed a hand down the wrinkled cotton. "Some shirts, too."

He made no attempt to disguise his reaction. The fierce satisfaction that flickered in his dark eyes prompted her to issue a caution.

"I'm not inviting you to move in, Luis. I'm merely suggesting we redraw the boundaries."

He lifted a hand and bushed a knuckle down her cheek. "I know what you're suggesting, *querida.* But you should know that these boundaries involve more than living arrangements. I want you to let me into your heart as well."

"I have," she said quietly. "I care for you. Deeply. You know that. And I know you care for me. We wouldn't have lasted this long if the feeling wasn't mutual."

"Care for? Is that how you described your feelings for David?" His glance went to the nightstand. "Did he…?"

He stopped. Narrowed his eyes. Swept the room.

"The photograph." His glance cut back to Claire. "You've put it away?"

"I moved it to the living room, where I won't see it every day. Nor will you."

It wasn't the unrestrained passion Luis wanted from her, but it was a step in the right direction. A significant step. The rest would come, he vowed, and soon. He had a foot in the door now. Literally and figuratively.

"I will bring a shaving kit and a change of clothes next time I come. Now let's have breakfast, yes? You rouse many appetites, Claire."

Her cell phone rang as she extracted a copper skillet from the rack above the stove.

She'd traded Luis's shirt for her celery-green caftan and had dragged a quick brush through her hair but hadn't progressed to the underwear or makeup stage yet. With a slither of silk, she dug her cell phone from her pocket and checked caller ID.

"Sorry, Luis. It's my answering service. I need to take it."

"Of course. While you do, I'll get the newspaper."

"Dr. Cantwell."

Frowning, Claire listened while her answering service relayed several messages from concerned clients. Apparently, they'd seen a report of the attack on the early-morning news. After requesting the service to assure all callers she'd sustained no injury, she disconnected.

"Apparently, we made the morning news," she told Luis as he walked in with the *Post*.

"Indeed we did."

Flipping the paper around, he displayed their photos printed side by side in the lower quadrant of the front page.

Claire shook her head. "I suppose I shouldn't be surprised. Even by Washington standards, a fatal incident involving a prominent psychologist and the Cartozan ambassador to the United States warrants at least passing interest. Does the story say anything about the identity of the attacker?"

He skimmed the lead-in and flipped to page 10C. "Either the police have not ID'ed him yet or they're withholding the identity pending notification of next of kin. I'll call Detective Waterman later and find out what he knows."

Claire's phone buzzed again while she stood behind Luis's chair, reading the story over his shoulder.

"Please hold for the president," an operator requested.

John Andrews came on the line a moment later. "I got word early this morning about the attack, Dr. Cantwell. They said you weren't hurt, but I wanted to make sure you're not suffering any aftereffects."

"I'm fine, sir."

"And Colonel Esteban? How is he this morning?"

She didn't ask how the president of the United States knew the colonel was sitting across the breakfast table from her.

They hadn't kept their relationship a secret. More to the point, she didn't doubt someone in the White House had already called the Cartozan embassy and discovered the ambassador had not returned to his residence last night.

"He's also well," she replied, and mouthed "the president" in answer to Luis's lifted brow.

"I've got to get congress to move on the sweeping anti-crime legislation I sent to the Hill my second month in office," Andrews said grimly. "The NRA has been lobbying behind the scenes to keep it buried in the House Subcommittee on Crime, Terrorism and Homeland Security. Hope you don't mind if I use you and the colonel as examples of why we as a nation have to implement drastic measures to regain control of our streets."

"I certainly don't mind. I'm sure Luis won't, either. Would you like to speak to him about it?"

"Tell him I'll have my people pass the request through official channels, along with my personal apologies that a member of the diplomatic corps was assaulted in our nation's capital. That'll put additional pressure on the subcommittee to get off their collective behinds."

"Glad we could be of service," Claire said dryly. "On another subject, what kind of night did Stacy have?"

"Not good." Frustration and worry colored the president's reply. "The nightmare hit about five a.m. I'd already heard about the mugging, so I told Tom Fogarty not to call you."

Claire blew out a slow breath. She was rapidly running out of options. Judging by the ragged edge to the president's voice, so was he.

"I think I'd better fly to Prague and talk to the archbishop," she told him. "Hopefully, he can help me get to the root cause of these nightmares."

"I'll instruct Tom to set up transportation. When do you want to leave?"

"This afternoon. I'll need the rest of the morning to clear my schedule."

And brief Lightning. Her boss at OMEGA needed to know the situation was rapidly escalating to crisis status.

"Any time after noon would be fine."

"Tom will contact you to confirm the arrangements. And Claire…?"

"Yes?"

"Thanks."

"You're welcome. Please tell Stacy I'll do my damnedest to find some answers over there."

Before she could hang up, her cell phone signaled

another call. The code that flashed across caller ID indicated it originated from OMEGA control.

If it was anyone but Luis sitting across the table, she would have excused herself to take both this call and the last. But he'd worked a number of ops with OMEGA agents, Claire included. He knew the organization and their charter almost as well as she did.

"This is Cyrene."

"Rigger here, Cyrene. Lightning asked if you could swing by sometime today."

"I was planning to stop in this morning. I need to give him an update on the Andrews situation. I also need to mission prep."

"You goin' somewhere we don't know about?"

"Prague. This afternoon. I'm not sure what airport we'll fly into. As soon as I know, you'll have to work the necessary clearances to get my weapon through security at their end."

"No problem. Anything else?"

"Not at the moment. Tell the boss I'll see him shortly."

"Will do."

She flipped the phone shut and smiled an appeal to Luis. "I have to shower, pack a quick bag and get my assistant to work juggling my schedule."

"So I heard."

"Why don't you fix breakfast for yourself? I'll

come downstairs again as soon as I'm dressed and packed."

He shook his head and pushed back his chair. "You have much to do today. So do I. That includes," he added, with a grin that showed a row of white teeth below his black mustache, "packing a spare shaving kit."

The grin made Claire suspect she'd opened a door she might find hard to close again. But as Luis drew her against him, she shrugged aside the vague wariness the thought generated.

"I shall see you when I see you, *querida*."

She returned the kiss, aroused by the feel of his mouth on hers, despite the multitude of tasks tugging at her mind.

Fifteen minutes after Luis departed, she'd showered and attacked her hair with a blow-dryer. A quick dusting of blush and a swipe of lip gloss sufficed for makeup before Claire threw a few things in an overnight bag.

The Baretta Px4 subcompact she kept in the nightstand drawer went into the special compartment sewn into her shoulder bag. She didn't anticipate needing the firearm, but no OMEGA agent ever departed on a mission unarmed. And after last night, the added weight of the pistol felt comfortingly familiar.

Miraculously, rush hour traffic had thinned enough for Claire to arrive at her office just as her assistant was unlocking the door. She departed an hour later with an appointment to speak with Cardinal Tuma the following afternoon. The incredibly efficient Mae Thompson also reserved a hotel room and rental car in Prague before taking on the daunting task of rescheduling a week's worth of appointments.

Claire drove from her office to OMEGA. While she was zipping down Massachusetts Avenue, Tom Fogarty called to advise her that an Air Force C-20 would be prepped and ready for her at Andrews Air Force Base at one o'clock.

"They've requested and have received clearance to land at Prague's International Airport. The crew has instructions to stand by for a return trip."

"Thanks."

Fogarty hesitated for a moment. "Are you sure this trip is necessary, Dr. Cantwell?"

Obviously, or she wouldn't be going!

"It's a long shot," Claire admitted coolly, "but worth checking out."

"The problem is, I'm not sure how much longer I can keep a lid on this situation. The media has a way of sniffing things out."

That was putting it politely. The paparazzi had hounded Claire unmercifully during her husband's short captivity and subsequent execution. She knew all too well how tenacious—and how intrusive—they could be.

"If they hear rumors and start running stories on Stacy's nightmares," Fogarty worried, "the president may be forced into a decision. God knows, he's got enough on his mind without this added worry."

"Let's hope it won't come to that. Just hold the fort for a few more days."

The urgency of the situation gnawed at Claire as she turned off Massachusetts Avenue and down a side street lined with chestnut trees still showing new green. Ordinarily, she'd park in the four-story garage on the next block. The garage gave onto a concealed entrance that led to OMEGA's high-tech control center. Since time was at a premium this morning, she pulled up in front of the Federal-style brick edifice with a discreet bronze plaque beside the door identifying it as home to the offices of the president's special envoy.

She was buzzed right in to Lightning's office. He listened with a grim expression while she updated him on last night's attack and her phone conversation with both the president and his chief of staff.

"Fogarty said he isn't sure how much longer he can keep this off the airwaves," she related. "He's worried that a media blitz about Stacy's condition may add to her stress, exacerbate the nightmares and force the president into a decision."

Lightning drummed his fingers on the polished surface of his desk. He looked every inch the wealthy executive this morning in his Italian silk tie and hand-tailored suit. Only a handful of OMEGA operatives knew this multimillionaire had once picked pockets to stay alive.

His next comment indicated he'd been mulling over a possibility that Claire herself had kicked around in the back of her mind. "Do you think last night's warning to back off could be connected to the situation at the White House?"

"I've considered that. No one outside the president's tight circle of advisors and a handful of his personal staff are aware that I'm working with Stacy. But you and I both know this town leaks like a sieve. One of the staff might have let something drop in the wrong place to the wrong person."

"A person—or persons—who would stand to gain if John Andrews did resign," Lightning said tersely. "That could include any number of special interests who've already been hit, and hit hard, by the president's wire-brush approach to re-prioritizing the budget."

With that grim possibility forefront in her mind, Claire took the titanium-shielded elevator to the third floor. She stepped out into a world of computers, wall-size screens and banks of the world's most sophisticated communications equipment.

Joe Devlin was on the desk again. "I'll act as your controller while you're in Prague," he assured her. "Whatever you need, just contact me."

"Will do."

"I've arranged clearance for you to carry your weapon through Czech security. Also a list of contacts you might find useful over there."

"Thanks."

As soon as the communications technician on duty synced the list to her cell phone, Claire whisked back down the elevator and got into her car for the drive across the Potomac to Andrews Air Force Base. The base was home to the eighty-ninth airlift wing, which provided presidential airlift support via Air Force One, as well as a fleet of helicopters and smaller executive jets. One of those was standing by to whisk her across the Atlantic and back.

Claire showed her credentials at the front gate and again at the access point for the restricted area of the flight line. She hurried to the operations area to check in, fully prepared for a long flight.

She *wasn't* prepared to find Luis Esteban in jeans, a crisp white shirt with the cuffs rolled up, and aviator sunglasses, waiting for her in the ops center.

Chapter 5

"Luis! What are you doing here?"

He gestured to the leather carryall on the floor beside him. "I'm flying to Prague with you."

"When did you decide that?"

"After I spoke with Detective Waterman."

His face settled into tight lines. Peeling off his aviator sunglasses, he hooked a stem through the open neck of his shirt.

"Waterman ID'd our attacker. His name—one of many he used—was Edward Porter."

Frowning, Claire searched a mental database of her case files. "I don't recognize the name."

"You would not. He's a professional killer. Detective Waterman indicated Porter may be behind a string of murder-for-hires. Until we know who hired him to attack you, you need someone to watch your back."

She stiffened and wavered between acknowledging the truth of that statement and annoyance that Luis had taken it upon himself to do the watching.

"You should have consulted me. If in fact I do need backup, OMEGA can provide it."

"That goes without saying. But I have a personal stake in protecting your so beautiful backside, *querida*. And in helping you uncover the cause of Stacy Andrews's nightmares. They began in my country. Until we know how and why, his daughter's condition may color how President Andrews deals with Cartoza."

Perhaps not the president, Claire thought, but most assuredly his chief of staff. She hadn't forgotten the terse exchange between Luis and Tom Fogarty on the White House lawn. She suspected Fogarty hadn't either.

Everything Luis said made sense. Yet, she couldn't shake the feeling he was pushing her too hard and too fast. Frowning, she made no effort to hide her displeasure as she concurred with something less than graciousness.

"Since you're so determined to tag along, I

won't stop you. But we play this op by my rules. Understood?"

He hooked a brow at her tone. "I would like to think of us as partners."

"I'm the one who has to report to the president," she reminded him, with a touch of ice in her voice. "This is my mission, Esteban. We do it my way, or not at all."

His dark eyes flashed with a temper to match hers, but he controlled it with an obvious effort.

"Very well. As long as *you* understand that *you* are my first priority, not your mission."

She should have been more grateful for his concern. More appreciative of his desire to watch her back. But she'd made the shift from psychologist to operative mode, and she didn't find his caveman attitude as amusing *or* as erotic as when he'd pulled it on her the other night.

With a curt nod, she strode past him to check in. The NCO manning the desk scrutinized her credentials and had her sign the manifest before making a request.

"We've got a couple of troops who need to get back to their base in Germany. We don't usually add passengers on presidential support aircraft, but one of the men is scheduled to depart for Iraq with his unit next week. Would you mind if we put them on your flight?"

"Not at all."

After adding the two soldiers to the manifest, the NCO escorted them, Luis and Claire out onto the tarmac. As Fogarty had promised, the Gulfstream III was prepped and ready to go. So was the five-person crew. The copilot and flight engineer were in the cockpit running preflight checklists, but the pilot had waited to introduce herself.

"Major Veronica Talbot, ma'am." The trim, honey-haired officer held out her hand. Her grip was firm and no-nonsense, her smile quick and lively. "Our estimated flying time to Prague is twelve and a half hours, with a brief touchdown at Ramstein AB, Germany, to refuel and offload our other passengers. I'll give you a better fix on our ETA once we get airborne."

She paused and flicked a glance at Claire's shoulder bag.

"I understand you're carrying a weapon aboard. You and the ambassador both."

Claire didn't wait for confirmation from Luis. As she knew well, he didn't go anywhere unarmed.

"That's correct," she said, answering for them both.

"Please remove the clip and make sure you don't have a round in the chamber before you board. We don't want to risk either weapon going off while we're in the air."

Claire had flown often enough on missions to know the drill, but she respected the pilot's safety concerns. Sliding a hand into her purse, she extracted the Baretta. Luis bent and unholstered his subcompact Glock.

Once the security check was completed, they mounted the steps to an interior fitted with a conference table and plush airline-style seats. With the ramp raised and the four passengers strapped in, Major Talbot joined her copilot in the cockpit to complete their final checklist. Soon the Gulfstream's twin Rolls Royce turbofan engines revved up to a high-pitched shriek. The jet rolled down the runway, gathering speed, and lifted off. Mere moments later, they were out over the Atlantic.

The presence of other passengers precluded any discussion between Claire and Luis of the reasons behind this flight. It didn't, however, prevent the colonel from engaging the two military men in a lively conversation.

Claire reclined her leather seat and stretched her legs. As she listened to their exchange, she forced herself to let go of her lingering resentment at Luis's high-handedness. Her mission was too important to allow negative emotions to cloud her thinking. Nor, she decided after considerable inner debate, could she allow the sensual heat this man stirred in her with a single touch to distract her.

* * *

She waited to inform Luis of that decision until they touched down at Ruzyne–Prague International Airport.

Although they'd made good time, with the stop in Germany and the six-hour time difference they landed at almost the same time they'd departed D.C., just a day later. Major Talbot taxied the military jet to the auxiliary airfield terminal reserved for smaller aircraft and parked in a spot outside the hangar that housed the Fixed Base Operations Center.

A wall of humidity hit Claire as she disembarked from the Gulfstream. Late spring had already transitioned to a hot, early summer in this corner of Eastern Europe. Feeling the heat, she turned to the pilot and held out her hand.

"Thanks for a smooth flight, Major."

"Our pleasure, Dr. Cantwell. We'll gas up and preflight for the return trip tomorrow morning, then go into crew rest."

"You're all set with a hotel?"

"Yes, ma'am." The pilot handed her a business card emblazoned with the seal of the eighty-ninth airlift wing. "Here's my cell phone number. Just call if there's any change to the schedule. Per instructions from the White House, we're at your complete disposal."

"You have my cell number?"

"Yes, ma'am. It's on the manifest. Ambassador Esteban's as well."

"Very good. We'll plan to depart tomorrow morning, unless something unforeseen occurs."

Which it did, a mere fifteen minutes later.

Thanks to the clearance Rigger had arranged, Claire whisked through both customs and immigration with no questions about the weapon in her shoulder bag. Luis's diplomatic passport afforded him the same preferential treatment.

After they'd tossed their bags in the trunk of the silver-gray Mercedes waiting in a reserved slot under Claire's name, she called Cardinal Tuma's office to confirm her appointment. Luckily, she'd made the appointment for late in the afternoon. With the detailed driving instructions the cardinal's efficient assistant had provided, she'd be able to arrive at his residence right on time.

Or not.

When Claire reached the cardinal's executive assistant, Father Milosec put a severe dent in her plans. "I regret to inform you, Dr. Cantwell," he said in heavily accented English, "his eminence suffered a sinking spell this morning."

"I'm sorry to hear that."

Extremely sorry.

"His doctor insists he rest for at least twenty-four hours. I've blocked a half hour for you at two tomorrow afternoon, if that is convenient."

It would have to be. Masking her disappointment at the delay, Claire confirmed the time.

"I'll be there at two o'clock. I hope his eminence has a restful night."

"We hope so, too. Many thousands of faithful will keep him in their prayers."

Disconnecting, Claire broke the news to Luis. "Cardinal Tuma is ill. We're on hold until tomorrow. I'd better notify the crew we're looking at a later departure."

Major Talbot took the delay in stride. "No problem, ma'am. I can think of a whole lot worse places to spend some down time than Prague. We'll notify our schedulers and stand by until we hear from you."

"She's right," Luis commented when Claire relayed the pilot's response. "There are far worse places to while away a few empty hours. Have you been to the city of a hundred spires before, *querida?*"

With a shake of her head, she backed out of the reserved slot. "It's one of the few places I haven't visited."

"Prague will enchant you," he promised once they cleared the exit and spotted the signs for the city center, "as it does all who visit the old town square or stroll across Charles Bridge at sunset."

"We're not here to stroll or play tourist, Luis."

The retort came out more sharply than Claire had intended. Blowing out a breath, she apologized.

"I'm sorry. It's just… This delay concerns me. There's so much riding on this trip."

"Indeed there is."

"Too much to allow our personal relationship to distract us from the business at hand," she said deliberately. "I think we should take separate rooms at the hotel."

She caught the glance he slid her and braced for a repeat of their somewhat heated discussion before they'd boarded the Gulfstream. Instead, Luis merely shrugged.

"Then it's just as well my staff also made reservations at the Savoy."

Claire wasn't surprised the embassy staff had ferreted out her hotel. They interacted frequently with her office manager to coordinate schedules, theater tickets and dinner engagements. What *did* surprise her was Luis's casual acceptance of separate rooms. She understood why when they checked into the elegant boutique hotel.

A member of the Leading Small Hotels of the World, the five-star Savoy was located in Prague's Upper Town, only steps from the castle and the magnificent cathedral that dominated the city.

After negotiating the city's narrow, twisting streets, Claire handed the keys to the Savoy's valet with heartfelt relief. A doorman escorted her and Luis through ornate glass doors, into a lobby tiled in exquisite marble and lit by crystal chandeliers. Beginning to feel the effects of the long flight and six-hour time differential, she slid her passport and American Express card across the reception counter.

"I'm Claire Cantwell. I have a reservation."

"Ah, yes. Welcome to the Savoy." The dignified clerk included Luis in his warm smile. "And you, Ambassador Esteban. We have the Royal Suite all ready for you and Dr. Cantwell."

"The Royal Suite?" Claire echoed.

"Yes, madam. The Cartozan Embassy confirmed the arrangements just this morning. You and the ambassador will be most comfortable."

Her brows drew together. "I believe my assistant reserved a deluxe room for me."

"Indeed she did, madam, but the embassy said… Er…"

The clerk looked to Luis, who stepped calmly into the breach.

"The suite has two bedrooms, does it not?"

"It does, sir, and two baths in addition to a large dining and sitting area."

"Where we may work uninterrupted, *querida*. We may as well turn this mixup to our advantage."

Irritated again, Claire considered insisting on her own room. Common sense won out. She and Luis routinely shared bodily fluids. They could certainly share a sitting and dining room.

Still, she didn't hesitate to voice her suspicion after the porter took them by private lift to a penthouse suite decorated with antiques and inch-thick Turkish carpets.

"Did you instruct your people to reserve this suite in both our names?"

"No. I did request a suite, however, and asked them to advise your assistant of the reservation. It appears our staffs weren't expecting your so absurd announcement that we must occupy separate beds. Nor was I."

Claire tossed her purse on a sofa table and thrust a hand through her hair. She was jet-lagged and wrinkled and in no mood to argue.

"I'm too tired to discuss boundaries again, Luis. We'll go with this arrangement—as long as you understand one shaving kit does not entitle you to muscle in on any more of my missions. Or have your people work my hotel reservations."

He whipped his head around. The long flight had left him with a heavy five o'clock shadow. In his jeans and white shirt with the rolled-up sleeves, he looked more like he belonged on a Harley than in a penthouse suite.

He hit back like a biker, too. Fast. Hard. A power punch to the gut. "What *does* it entitle me to, Claire? Two nights a week in your bed? Three?"

"If you're going to reduce our relationship to that equation," she replied icily, "we might as well call it off right now."

He stiffened, and Claire gave herself a swift mental kick. How clumsy of her! How incredibly stupid!

This was no time to throw down a gauntlet. Not with everything riding on her mission. The last thing either of them needed was an emotional eruption.

"I'm sorry. That was unfair. I know you want more, Luis. So do I, but I have to take this one step at a time."

She waited, wondering if he'd accept the olive branch. After a small silence, he made a visible effort to rein in his anger.

"You are taking it one very careful, very cautious step at a time."

"I know."

The rest of his anger left him on a gust of breath. Shaking his head, he curled a knuckle under her chin.

"You embody such contradictions, my darling. You are so calm and insightful with your clients. So skilled and deadly in the field. So passionate with me, yet so wary of surrendering your heart."

She couldn't argue with that. Having said heart ripped out of her chest once would make anyone wary.

On the other hand, Luis hadn't exactly surrendered *his* heart, either. He made no secret of the fact he admired her enormously on an intellectual level and lusted for her physically. Yet, neither of them had whispered the dreaded *L* word.

Claire knew she was still a challenge to him. A citadel to conquer. And once he had...?

"Here is my suggestion," he said. "We shower, we rest, and then you let me show you Prague. It rivals Paris, I think, as one of the world's most romantic cities."

"Deal. Which bedroom do you want?"

His mouth curved in a wry smile. "You still insist on this?"

"I do."

He bowed and swept an arm toward the adjoining bedrooms. "Then you choose. I care not where I sleep, if it is not beside you."

* * *

"You're right," Claire breathed several hours later. "This city is incredible."

They'd followed a gently sloping walk to the lower gardens of the castle that dominated Prague's skyline. With elbows propped on a low stone parapet, she drank in the sight of the older sections of the city spread out below them.

"It really does have a hundred spires," she murmured in awe as her gaze swept a panoramic vista of slate roofs, turrets and tall, slender steeples.

The River Vlata curved directly below them, and bisected the city into neat halves. On either side of its banks, Gothic and Romanesque towers rose above narrow streets crowded with medieval buildings. Luis pointed to one tower, a massive structure thrusting up into the sky some blocks from the square, at the heart of Old Town.

"That is the Powder Gate, so called because it used to store gunpowder. It was one of the thirteen gates that guarded the king's castle and the city center, before the royal residence was moved up here to higher ground." His voice took on the caressing tone of a connoisseur's true love of beauty. "And that, *querida,* is the Karlov Möst. The Charles Bridge."

She followed his outswept arm to the world-famous bridge that connected the historic centers

of Prague. It was closed to vehicle traffic, allowing crowds of pedestrians to stroll across its sixteen graceful spans. Larger-than-life-size statues
adorned each span and gazed down from tall
marble pillars. Below the statues, street vendors
sketched caricatures of tourists, musicians sang to
the accompaniment of accordions and mandolins,
and artisans displayed hand-crafted jewelry or
clothing or religious artifacts.

"Are you up to walking across the bridge to Old
Town Square?" Luis asked.

"Definitely!"

A quick shower had reenergized Claire. That,
and the fact that the blast of humidity that had
smacked them in the face when they first arrived
had now tapered to a bearable warmth. Thank-
fully, she'd checked the weather before packing
and had included flat-heeled sandals and a sleeveless, lemon-colored tank she could dress up or
down. Arm in arm, she and Luis descended the
narrow streets of Upper Town and passed through
the medieval gate that guarded the bridge.

"We must come across again tomorrow, early
in the morning," he told her. "Before the vendors
set up and the tourists crowd onto the bridge.
Seeing the mists swirl about the statues on Karlov
Möst with no one else present is to see Prague's
very essence."

Claire believed him, although she found the crowds invigorating and the musicians entertaining. Particularly the organ grinder decked out in a straw boater and red-striped shirt. While he pumped out tunes on his hand-cranked grinder, his trained monkey hopped at the end of a long leash to collect the coins tourists dropped in his tin cup.

Claire added a couple of euros to the cup before she and Luis continued their meandering. They paused with other tourists to rub the plaque identifying one of the statues as St. John of Nepomuk.

"It will bring luck," Luis asserted solemnly as he caressed the shiny spot on the plaque. "And bring you back to Prague."

Claire certainly hoped so. Everything she'd seen so far enchanted her. She gave the plaque a determined rub before strolling with Luis through the turreted tower guarding the far side of the bridge.

It gave onto a maze of cobbled streets with narrow, three- and four-story buildings crowded so close together they blocked the sun. Their varying architectural styles provided a feast for Claire's eyes. She craned her neck in an effort to absorb details on facades that covered the spectrum from square, solid Romanesque to medieval Gothic to the incredibly intricate Renaissance, baroque and rococo periods.

Shops occupied the ground floor of many buildings. Elaborate signs above the doors identified each shop's specialty or trade. A fat, iron pig swung above the entrance to a restaurant with an outdoor menu that advertised stewed pigs' knuckles, braised ham and grilled pork roast. An apothecary's mortar and pestle designated a drug store with a window display featuring everything from aspirin to Xylocaine.

Enthralled by the sights and sounds and tantalizing scents that filled the air, Claire almost missed the tiny bookshop wedged between a bakery and a store with a display of sparkling Czech crystal.

"Luis!" She dragged him to a halt and pointed to a collection of leather-bound volumes. "Look at those antique guidebooks."

She barely gave him time to glance at the items before reaching for the doorknob. A bell tinkled merrily as she stepped across the threshold. The scent of old leather and musty pages tickled her nostrils.

The elderly shopkeeper glanced up at their entrance and peered at them over his rimless glasses. *"Blaho odpoledne."*

Claire took that as a greeting and smiled. "Good afternoon."

"Ah, you are English."

"American."

"Welcome to my store. How may I help you?"

"I'd like to see one of the antique guidebooks in the window."

"Yes, yes, show me the one."

They moved to the window and Claire pointed to a slim volume, so old the leather had flaked off in several places. When she held the volume in her hands, Luis read the title over her shoulder.

"An Englishman's Walking Guide to the Ghouls and Spectral Haunts of Prague."

Carefully, Claire opened to a yellowed page. The hand-drawn illustration on the page stopped her breath in her throat.

A caped and hooded skeleton stared back at her with black, empty sockets. The grim specter gripped a rosary in its boney right hand. Its left was wrapped around the long wooden handle of a scythe.

On impulse, Claire turned to the bookstore owner. "Do you by any chance have a copy of a treatise written by Cardinal Tuma fifty years ago? One that also deals with skeletons and apparitions?"

"I have heard of this work," the shopkeeper replied. "But I have never seen a copy in print."

Disappointed, Claire purchased the slender volume. She and Luis left the bookstore a little later with the guidebook wrapped in brown paper and tucked inside her shoulder bag. If nothing else, it might give her some insight into the Slavic mentality Cardinal Tuma had written about in his treatise.

"I'll read it tonight," she told Luis. "Maybe we can visit some of the spots in the guide tomorrow, before our appointment with the cardinal."

As the evening sun painted the ancient buildings with a golden glow, and strolling crowds filled the sidewalk cafés and restaurants, Claire had no inkling she would wake screaming in terror before the night was done.

Chapter 6

For weeks and months afterward, Claire would try to retrace the hours leading up to the horrifying dream.

She felt no premonition, no sense of any pending cataclysmic event while she and Luis ambled through the summer twilight. As he'd predicted, Prague thoroughly enthralled her. History practically oozed through the walls of the buildings looming over cobbled streets. Everywhere she looked, she found another architectural gem.

Mullioned bow windows straight out of the fourteenth or fifteenth century. Ancient wells crowned with lacy ironwork and strategically placed for generations of city dwellers to draw their water. Gorgeously painted facades. The soaring twin spires of the Church of Our Lady Before Tyn, which dominated one side of Old Town's main square— arguably one of the most beautiful in Europe.

But it was Prague's unique astronomical clock that cemented her love affair with the city. She and Luis joined the crowd that gathered every hour on the hour in the square, facing the southern wall of the Old Town city hall. A festive mood filled the air as tourists snapped pictures of each other standing under the massive clock or feasted on sausages and pilsner in the surrounding outdoor cafés.

Claire and Luis were lucky enough to snag a table directly across from the clock. She let him place an order for two pilsners, bowing to his superior knowledge of brands and labels. She sipped the pale beer and listened in amusement while he waxed eloquent on a subject he'd obviously researched firsthand.

"Czechs have been brewing beer in Pilsen and Budweis since the eleventh century."

"Budweis? As in Budweiser?"

"Exactly. The Czechs were the first to produce a light, golden brew. It became so popular they exported it extensively to other countries. At one point, a special beer train left Pilsen for Vienna every morning. The Germans soon learned their brewing secrets, and it was a German immigrant who set up the Budweiser Brewing Company in the U.S."

He downed a healthy swallow and rolled his lips to erase the foam on his mustache.

"Not surprisingly, Czechs consume more beer per capita than any other population on earth. Something like three hundred pints a year. It would be interesting to see how that compares to wine consumption in France, or overall alcohol consumption in the U.S., yes?"

Claire had a good idea how it would compare. She dealt with the effects of alcohol abuse regularly in her practice. Unfortunately, alcoholism rates among adults and binge drinking among teens were rising steadily each year in the U.S., as well as Europe.

She didn't want to dwell on those grim statistics right now, though. Not with the flaming ball of the sun about to drop behind Prague's magical spires and Luis sitting across from her, looking so damned sexy in his fresh, open-neck shirt and well-worn jeans that every woman passing by the outdoor café did a double take.

The sonorous bong of a bell instantly diverted her attention to the two circular faces of the huge astronomical clock. The top face contained the astrolabe, an intricate series of dials that tracked the movement of the sun and moon and displayed various zodiac symbols. The bottom face, added in later centuries, displayed the months in a gorgeously ornate calendar.

Anticipation rippled through the crowd as the bell chimed the hour. Claire propped her chin in her palms, then watched with breathless fascination as carved wooden statues of the twelve apostles appeared one by one in the doors above the clock. At the same time, the four statues flanking it began to move forward.

How incredible that such precision and beauty could have been created so many centuries ago. Especially with the wars and plagues that regularly swept across continents. Life expectancy back then could be measured in two or three decades.

Sitting in the café, listening to the sonorous chimes, Claire suspected each strike of the hour not only told the time, it reminded mortals to repent their sins, as their time on earth was short.

Or, as she had suggested to Stacy, was this a visible reminder to Prague's citizens to focus on what was good in life instead of the bad? The joy instead of the sorrows? The future instead of the past…?

Her glance shifted to the man beside her. She'd taken a major step toward letting go of *her* past by removing Dave's picture from her bedroom, and another huge step by inviting Luis to share that bedroom on a more frequent basis.

Why couldn't she take the next step? What held her back from total commitment? Remembered pain? Guilt? The sneaking, insidious thought that, as long as she represented a challenge, she'd keep Luis on the hook?

God, she hoped she wasn't that shallow or manipulative! Still, she felt somewhat subdued until the astronomical clock completed its bonging and Luis turned to her.

"Shall we have dinner here in Old Town? I know a place that serves the best fried pork dumplings I've eaten."

Nodding, Claire gathered her things. "Fried pork dumplings sound wonderful."

Dusk had given way to a starry summer sky by the time they finished. Claire soon realized that while Prague by day was incredible, night made the city magical.

Floodlights gave a stunningly dramatic view of the castle and St. Vitus Cathedral high on the hill across the river. Not even the presence of scaffolding could detract from the sight of the spires silhouetted against an ink-black sky. In Old Town, more floods illuminated the facades of the buildings lining the square. Wrought-iron lamps transformed the Charles Bridge into a softly lit lovers lane where couples ambled arm in arm.

Luis and Claire strolled back across the bridge under the watchful eye of the bishops and saints mounted on their pedestals. An electric tram transported them up the steep hill to Upper Town and let them off a mere half block from the Savoy.

Once in their suite, the stunning view of the castle and cathedral drew Claire to the wide terrace that ran the length of the palatial suite. She heard a clink of crystal behind her, and Luis emerged a moment later with a brandy snifter cradled in each palm.

"Magnificent, is it not?"

"And then some," she agreed.

She accepted a heavy crystal snifter and held it up as Luis did the same with his.

"To us," he said, with a look that somehow managed to convey amusement, wry acceptance and undisguised desire, "one very careful step at a time."

"To us."

Claire savored the brandy's smoky bite, sipping slowly. Luis leaned his elbows next to hers on the wide stone railing and did the same. Neither mentioned their sleeping arrangements, but Claire knew the issue had to be on his mind as much as it was on hers.

She'd made the right decision by insisting they occupy separate beds on this op. As much as she'd enjoyed the afternoon and evening with Luis, she needed to be clear and focused tomorrow. She also had to work through this nagging sense that he was pushing her too far, too fast.

Sternly, she suppressed the traitorous thought that a bout of hot, sweaty sex might be *exactly* what she needed to blow the doubts out of her head. She'd made her bed. Tonight, at least, she'd lie in it.

When Luis moved a little away and extracted the inevitable cigarillo from a silver case, she used that as a cue to make a graceful exit.

"I think I'll curl up and read the book we bought while you enjoy your cigar." She moved in enough to lay a palm against his cheek. "I'll see you in the morning."

He bent his head to take the kiss she offered. His mouth was warm, his mustache silky against her upper lip. Claire carried the taste of him on her lips to the bedroom she'd chosen.

Luis's glance trailed her as she went through the French doors. He knew he'd pushed her close to the line by muscling in on this trip to Prague. He'd invaded her space both physically and mentally. It didn't take a PhD to recognize that Claire's insistence on separate bedrooms was her attempt to restore the delicate balance of power.

Recognizing that fact, however, didn't necessarily mean Luis had to like it. Or accept it.

Torn by conflicting urges, he lit his cigar and pulled in the taste of rum-soaked tobacco. Every primal instinct he possessed shouted at him to kick open her bedroom door and stake his claim once and for all. Only the thin veneer of civilization, crafted by education and society, held him back. That, and the absolute certainty Claire would use the same lethal moves on him as she had on their attacker.

Porter. Edward Porter.

Luis's stomach knotted at the memory of the knife the bastard had held to Claire's throat. Frowning, he racked his mind for a connection, any connection, to the warning to back off that Porter had whispered in her ear.

Was it him? Had *he* drawn the attack and the warning? God knows, he'd made his share of enemies as Cartoza's chief of security. The leaders of at least three drug cartels operating out of neighboring Colombia had put a bounty on his head.

His jaw working, Luis rolled the cigarillo from one corner of his mouth to the other.

The shapes came at her out of the darkness. Amorphous. Indistinct. Shrouded in swirls of mist that felt icy cold on her skin. They seemed to drag forward, weighted down by a universe of worry, of fear.

Closer they came. And closer. Until the mist

parted and she could see some in dresses topped with dingy aprons, others in baggy pants and homespun shirts. And there! A mincing popinjay in bright silks! She was trying to take in his ruffled cuffs and knee britches worn above high-heeled, buckled shoes, when another figure emerged from the crowd. She couldn't see his face, couldn't see any of their faces clearly, but the set of his shoulders triggered something. Some memory. Some primal recognition.

Her joy was instant, liquid and molten, filling every corner of her being. She held out her arms, crying to him.

Dave! Dave!

He moved closer, part of the crowd that flowed around her. She could almost see his face now, almost make out his features. Her heart beat so hard and fast she could hear it, feel it hammering against her ribs.

Dave!

She tried to run to him but her legs wouldn't move. Tried to call out to him but her cry became a low, agonized mewl as his features, still indistinct, blurred even more. Slowly, so slowly, the pale oval of his face began to disintegrate.

No! Dear God, no! Don't leave me! Not again!

Helpless, unable to move, she writhed with a grief so sharp it stabbed into her heart like a surgeon's knife. Before her eyes everything that was Dave, everything that had been her husband, melted away. His clothing, his tall, muscular frame, his very being.

Until all that remained were bones. A skull staring at her with empty, soulless eyes. A collection of bones moving as if by wire. Coming toward her. Reaching for her.

She backed away. Heard an ominous rattle. Spun in a circle to find herself ringed by macabre skeletons. All reaching for her. All moving toward her. Pulling her hair. Tearing her clothes. Peeling away her flesh.

She fought back. Fought Dave. Fought them all. Kicking, biting. Flailing her fists. She couldn't stop them. Their bony fingers as sharp as talons, they tore the flesh from her face.

The scream jolted Luis awake.

In a move as instinctive as it was swift, he rolled out of bed and grabbed his ankle holster from the nightstand. He didn't stop to pull on his jeans. Yanking the Glock out of the holster, he raced for Claire's room.

Another scream ripped through the night. His veins icing, Luis cocked the pistol on the run. He burst through the door to Claire's room and dropped into a crouch. Enough light came through the transom over the drawn drapes for him to sweep the room. Two seconds later, he surged upright and hit the light switch.

The sight of Claire tangled in the covers, thrashing back and forth as she clawed the air, put an icy chill dead center in his heart.

"Jesu!"

Shoving his weapon onto the bedside table beside the slim volume they'd purchased earlier, he caught her wildly flailing wrists.

"Claire! *Mi amor!*"

"No! No!"

"It's Luis. I am here."

She fought him, astounding him with her strength. He had to exert a good deal of effort to maintain his grip on this slender, delicate woman.

"You're dreaming. Claire, do you hear me? You're dreaming. Wake up, my darling."

Her eyelids flew up. She stared at him, her pupils huge, dark pools of terror.

"Lu…?" She slicked her tongue over dry, cracked lips. "Luis?"

"Yes." He eased his brutal hold. "I'm here."

The fight went out of her, but not the horror. Her eyes were wild. Shudders racked her entire body.

With a muttered oath, he released her wrists and yanked away the constricting covers so he could slide into bed beside her. When he took her in his arms, she collapsed against his naked chest. Her hands clutched desperately at his arms, her nails dug deep into his biceps.

He held her. Just held her. Stroking her hair. Murmuring words of comfort and assurance. Feeling helpless and alarmed and shaken to his core by the violent tremors she transmitted from her body to his.

He couldn't gauge how long it took for her terror to fade. A good ten or fifteen minutes, he guessed, although it seemed like hours. Eventually the shudders ceased and she dug her nails out of his upper arms.

Still he held her, waiting while her breathing steadied and the quiet of the night settled around them. When she finally angled her head and met his gaze, the unspeakable tragedy in her eyes grabbed him by the throat.

"It was Dave," she whispered. "I dreamed about Dave. He… He melted away right before my eyes."

Luis certainly didn't have the wall full of degrees Claire did, but he could make the connection.

"I understand," he murmured, aching for her even as he kicked himself for urging her to take steps she obviously wasn't ready for. "To accommodate me you moved David out of your bedroom, literally and perhaps figuratively. Now guilt has hit you. With a vengeance."

She pushed a little off his chest. A deep crease

formed between her brows. She was still shaken, still troubled, but the Claire he knew had already emerged from the terrified woman of a few minutes ago.

"This was more than a manifestation of suppressed guilt. His *flesh* just melted away. Right before my eyes. Like in Stacy Andrews's nightmares."

Another shudder rippled through her.

"Dave wasn't the only one in the dream," she told him slowly. "There were others. A great many others. Strange people dressed in strange clothes. Surrounding me. The flesh shredded off their bones, until they were all skeletons reaching for me and ripping at *my* flesh."

Listening to her, Luis felt an instinctive urge to make a hasty sign of the cross. And he couldn't remember the last time he'd done that!

Like most Central Americans, he'd been born and raised a Catholic. But he'd seen too much of the brutal and deranged to sustain a belief in the goodness of man or a benevolent God. His world was too dark, too vicious—or had been until he'd met Claire.

But the old beliefs apparently went deep. So deep he found himself formulating a silent, instinctive prayer for help in keeping his woman safe from all evil.

"It's a classic case of transference." With a ragged sigh, she dropped back down on his chest. "I've been so obsessed with Stacy's nightmares, spent so many hours analyzing them and trying to find their source. I guess I shouldn't be surprised they would invade my subconscious as well."

Luis wasn't quite ready to accept the rational explanation. Not after seeing the stark terror in her eyes. He wrapped his arms around her, holding her close again, while she talked through her residual fright.

"It probably didn't help to read that guidebook we bought just before I fell asleep," she murmured against his chest. "According to the author, Prague has more than its share of ghouls and ghosts. The restless undead apparently prowl at will. Did you know Prague Castle is haunted?"

Luis visualized the vast complex of palaces, courtyards and cathedrals that seemed to float above the city. "I'm not surprised such tales arise, considering that the cathedral contains the relics of many saints. And as I recall, generations of Prague's royal family are entombed in the castle crypt."

"The royal family plays a major role in some of the legends," Claire murmured, with a glance at the guidebook lying facedown on the nightstand beside his Glock. "Supposedly, the four wives of Emperor Charles IV wander through their dank crypt at night, fighting among themselves and hoping for a last glimpse of their husband. Then there's the ghost of Saint John of Nepomuk."

"The saint on the Charles Bridge, whose plaque we rubbed for luck?"

"That's the one. According to legend, he heard the confession of Queen Johanna, wife of King Wenceslas the third or fourth."

She nudged her cheek against his chest, seeming to relax with the telling of these old tales. Luis held her loosely and let her ramble on.

"When St. John refused to divulge what sins the queen confessed, this not-so-good King Wenceslas had him tortured and thrown from the bridge. Supposedly, John wandered the surrounding area for nearly three hundred years before his soul found a home in the statue erected in his honor."

Her words grew slower, her voice a little sleepy.

"There are other ghosts," she murmured, rubbing her cheek against his chest again. "Ten lords who had their heads cut off and stuck on poles on the bridge. People swear they've heard their mournful cries carried on the wind at night."

Luis swallowed an oath. Until this moment, he'd revered the medieval bridge for its beauty and romance. Now he'd think of severed heads and tortured priests every time he strolled its graceful Gothic spans.

"No wonder you had such dreams," he muttered, casting a disapproving eye on the guidebook.

"There are more stories," she said sleepily. "You should read the one about the lost souls who wander each night in Prague's Jewish cemetery."

He didn't need to read it. He'd visited the old Jewish Quarter and could easily imagine ghosts drifting among the hundreds of tilting, moss-covered gravestones. Irrationally relieved that the overhead light was still on to chase away the shadows, he stroked Claire's hair.

"Enough of these tales. Sleep now, *querida*. Tomorrow we speak with the cardinal, yes? And then we go home."

Shooting the slim volume a last, evil look, Luis cradled Claire in his arms through the rest of the night.

Chapter 7

By the next morning, Claire had recovered her customary calm. Luis, on the other hand, continued to feel the aftereffects of her horrific nightmare.

He studied her as he sat across from her at a late breakfast. They'd had room service deliver it. At Claire's request, the waiter had set up a table on the terrace. The weather was perfect for eating outside. The muggy heat of yesterday had given way to a balmy spring morning. Tender green leaves rustled in the trees lining the square below, while a little more than a block away, the cathedral spires rose above castle ramparts and speared into a cloudless blue sky.

The setting couldn't have been more tranquil or the meal better prepared. Fragrant steam rose from a heavy silver coffeepot. Domed trays yielded eggs poached with white asparagus and succulent ham steaks. Claire had consumed both with her usual appetite, but the acid rolling around in Luis's stomach had him laying down his fork after only a couple of bites.

Seeing her so terrified had shaken him badly. *Still* shook him. Claire was normally so contained, so in control of her thoughts and emotions. She'd stripped herself bare last night, and Luis had yet to understand his reaction to that very different Claire. Somehow, some way, her terror had altered the delicate balance between them and made his heart trip with unfamiliar emotions.

The fierce protectiveness he felt toward her wasn't new. He was a man, and a very basic one at that. He made no apologies for the fact that both instinct and inclination conditioned him to protect those near and dear to him.

But this gut-wrenching ache to keep her safe from all fears… The wish that he could erase every last vestige of the pain of her husband's death… The growing conviction she had somehow become the center of his universe… That he couldn't envision his world without her…

These feelings were so intense, so all-consuming, his hand shook when he reached for his cup. Coffee slopped over the rim and splattered on the snowy tablecloth. Smothering a curse, he dabbed at the stain with his napkin.

"Luis?"

He glanced up to find Claire's gaze on him. No trace of her tumultuous night showed on her face. Not a single, pale gold strand of hair was out of place. Unlike him, she appeared to have put the episode completely out of her mind.

"Are you all right?" she asked, searching his face.

He hesitated, not quite ready to confess the emotions churning in his gut. He had to sort through them first. Try to understand when and how he'd made the jump from simply wanting this woman to wanting everything she had to give.

Burying his feelings, he shrugged. "I read portions of your guidebook while you were in the shower. I'm not surprised you woke screaming."

Carefully, Claire laid down her fork. The invigorating shower and the bright, sunny morning had gone a long way toward blunting the aftereffects of the horrific dream. Her main concern now was Luis.

He must have spent the entire night—or what was left of it after he'd burst into her room—stroking and soothing her. She remembered his warmth and the bone-deep reassurance she drew from the feel of his arms around her. Remembered as well the comfort she derived from his mere presence.

He, on the other hand, looked like he'd spent the hours until dawn battling the very demons that had frightened her. His eyes showed a tinge of red, and not even his crisp blue cotton shirt and knife-pleated tan slacks could disguise the tension cording his body.

"Did you get any sleep at all last night?" she asked, with an apologetic smile.

"Not much."

"I'm sorry."

"You have nothing to apologize for. I, however…" His handsome face troubled, he reached across the table to grasp her hand. "I would not hurt you for the world, Claire."

"I know that."

"If I have pushed you too hard," he said, holding her eyes with his, "if in my arrogance, I caused you pain or precipitated the guilt that triggered your nightmare, I am sorry."

Touched by his gruff apology, she turned her hand over and threaded her fingers through his.

"Yes, you've pushed too hard," she said with a wry smile. "And yes, you're incredibly arrogant. I'm learning how to deal with both. As for the guilt…" Her smile faded, but she didn't look away. "I'll work through it."

Eventually.

She hoped.

Luis accepted her quiet statement with a squeeze of her hand and let the matter drop.

"We still have several hours until the appointment with Cardinal Tuma. What do you wish to do until then?"

She'd already dressed for the coming interview in a slim back skirt and short-sleeve, scoop-neck ivory silk blouse, with ties that looped into a loose bow. Her low-heel pumps were both comfortable and stylish, and would have made for easy walking. As much as Claire would have liked to let Luis show her more of this fascinating city, the urgency behind their visit to Prague took precedence.

"I'd better review my case notes before we meet with the cardinal."

"Then I shall make use of the hotel's spa and exercise room," he said, pushing away from the table. "First I'll call down for a late checkout, yes? We can leave our bags with the concierge while we walk to the castle."

A hard workout in the Savoy's lavishly appointed gym helped Luis sweat out some of the stress from the night before. A deep-muscle massage by a semi-sadistic masseuse kneaded away the rest.

By the time he and Claire set out to walk the few blocks to the maze of buildings and battlements that comprised Prague Castle, he felt almost relaxed. Which didn't explain the odd feeling that gripped him when they strolled past sentries in ornate period uniforms and passed under a massive stone arch leading to one of the castle's courtyards. The sensation was barely perceptible. A slight, almost indiscernible tingling at the base of his skull that drifted down his spine, inch by slow inch.

Eyes narrowing, Luis tightened his grip on Claire's elbow and skimmed a glance around the cobbled courtyard. It was as long as two football fields. Ornate palaces ringed it on three sides. Some housed museums, others the offices of the president of the Czech Republic and various government departments.

The massive bulk of St. Vitus Cathedral dominated the fourth side of the courtyard. The seat of the archbishop of Prague, the towering Gothic structure had served as the burial place of saints and emperors for centuries. Bohemian kings had been crowned there for more than six hundred years, and their crown jewels still occupied a secure vault in the cathedral's southern vestibule. Not even the scaffolding marching all the way up to its spires could detract from its Gothic beauty.

Given its historic significance, Prague Castle

drew hoards of visitors. Tourists waited in long, roped-off lines to enter the cathedral. More queued up at the various museums on the castle grounds. Others chattered in a dozen different languages as they snapped pictures in front of fountains and elaborate facades. Laughing teens trailed after long-suffering teachers attempting to instill a sense of history in adolescents more interested in sex than medieval architecture.

Luis saw nothing in the crowds to account for the tension now gathered at the base of his spine. Maybe it was the noise. The marble facades of palaces surrounding the courtyard magnified and bounced back every sound. Added to that was the intermittent rattle of jackhammers. Their nerve-crunching blasts signaled the repair work necessitated after the earthquake that had rocked Prague last year.

The palace of the archbishop of Prague looked as though it, too, had sustained damage. Scaffolding almost obscured the entire front of the residence. The steel superstructures crawled up the elaborate rococo facade and encased the statues crowning the four-story building. Still frowning, Luis craned his neck. He spotted two plasterers repairing an arch over a window and what might have been a third worker moving among the statues.

Nothing to account for this odd sensation, yet

Luis couldn't shake it. Nor could he ignore it. He'd lived on the edge too long to dismiss any signal, however subtle. He was still trying to pinpoint its source when he and Claire walked through the tunnel in the scaffolding that led to the palace's front entrance. Once inside, the sheer magnificence of the reception hall drove everything else from his mind.

"Madre de Dios!"

Luis's travels had led him to a number of the world's great palaces. Versailles. Schönbrunn. Rambagh in Jaipur. The monumental Winter Palace, now the Hermitage Museum in St. Petersburg. One sweeping glance told him the archbishop of Prague lived amid almost as much splendor as any tsar or maharajah ever had.

There was marble everywhere—rich Carrera marble veined with gold. The furnishings in the reception hall had to have been bought or plundered centuries ago, while light poured over them through leaded windows two stories high.

They were greeted just inside the entrance by a security guard who confirmed their appointment before handing them over to a uniformed guide.

"Father Milosec is waiting for you. Please, come with me."

Their footsteps echoing on marble floors, they followed the guide through a series of public antechambers to a gallery lined with portraits of past bishops. That opened onto a second gallery containing sumptuous seventeenth-century tapestries that could only have been woven by Gobelin.

The private residence of the archbishop of Prague occupied the rear wing of the building. The rooms were somewhat less cavernous but still magnificent. With a smile and a bow, the guide ushered them into a suite of offices.

The cardinal's executive assistant rose and came around from behind his desk to shake their hands. Tall and stoop-shouldered, Father Milosec wore the old-style black cassock Luis remembered from the padres of his youth.

"I hope Cardinal Tuma is feeling better," Claire said when they'd exchanged greetings.

"He is," the priest replied in heavily accented English. "Unfortunately, his eminence's health is quite precarious these days. He's looking forward to your visit, however. This way, if you please."

After the majesty of the rest of the palace, Luis half expected to be shown into a gilded throne room. Instead, Father Milosec opened the door to a book-lined library redolent with the scent of wax candles and old parchment.

"The cardinal will offer his hand," the priest murmured as they entered. "It is the tradition to kneel and kiss his ring, even if you are not of our faith."

Claire nodded, and the priest raised his voice.

"Dr. Cantwell is here, Your Eminence, and Colonel Luis Esteban."

The tiny, silver-haired figure, huddled in a black cassock piped with red, looked up from the volume he'd been reading and murmured in Czech.

"His eminence welcomes you both," Milosec translated.

The cardinal offered a liver-spotted hand adorned by a heavy gold ring. Claire went down on one knee to kiss it. Luis did the same before moving to one of the chairs the cardinal indicated with a nod of his head.

With Father Milosec translating, Claire reiterated the urgency of her visit. "Thank you for agreeing to see me on such short notice. I very much appreciate it, as does our president. He's deeply concerned over his daughter's nightmares."

"Tell me of these dreams," the cardinal said through his assistant.

While Claire recounted the dreams' macabre elements, Luis's respect for her deepened. No one listening to this calm, collected professional would guess she'd suffered almost the same terrifying nightmare as her young client only hours ago.

When she finished, the cardinal sighed.

"Death, as represented by skeletal apparitions, plays often in the dreams of Slavs," he confirmed through his interpreter. "We have a morbid fascination with it, perhaps because we've seen so much of war and plague and pestilence throughout our history. This is what I wrote so many years ago in my treatise."

"Did you find these apparitions to recur frequently in dreams of specific individuals?"

"In many instances."

"What was the incident rate among young people?"

"I don't know that I ever calculated precise figures…." His forehead wrinkling, the cardinal searched his memory. "As I recall, the tendency was more common among children who had lost a parent to illness or war."

"Like Stacy Andrews," Claire murmured.

"You say the girl's great-grandfather came from Bohemia?"

"Yes, Your Eminence."

"Then such dreams may well run in her blood," the elderly cleric said sadly.

Father Milosec spoke up then. "Do you know the grandfather's name?"

The time Claire had spent going over her case notes this morning paid off. She answered without hesitation.

"Teodore Cernak. According to President Andrews, Cernak was conscripted into the Nazi navy at the age of sixteen, deserted and stowed away on a cargo ship bound for the States. Since there's no official record of his entry into the States, I haven't been able to pinpoint exactly where he was born or emigrated from."

"Perhaps I might be of help with that." A hint of pride crept into Father Milosec's voice. "I recently led the effort to computerize all parish records within our archbishopric. Some go back as far as the Middle Ages."

After asking permission from the cardinal, he moved to a marble desk supported by four carved lions and picked up a sleek digital phone. The irony of twenty-first-century technology cloaked in the rich pageantry of bygone eras wasn't lost on Luis.

Claire and Cardinal Tuma conversed for another five or ten minutes, but the cardinal could offer no suggestions for banishing Stacy's nightmares except prayer.

"It is a most powerful tool."

"It is indeed, Your Eminence."

Masking her disappointment, Claire went down on one knee again to kiss his ring. Luis knelt as well. When they emerged from the library, they discovered Father Milosec's pride in his computerization project was well justified. The lay clerk he'd called was waiting in the outer office with a printout. With a few hearty words of praise for the man's efforts, the priest translated for his guests.

"Teodore Cernak, son of Anya and Karel Cernak. Born 1923, in the parish of The Church of All Saints, Sedlec, Southern Bohemia. Ahhh, that may explain much!"

Claire immediately pounced. "How so?"

"Sedlec is a small town about an hour east of Prague. It is quite famous for its ossuary."

"Ossuary, as in a repository for human bones?"

"Exactly. The present-day Church of All Saints was built on the site of an eleventh-century Cistercian monastery. The monastery's abbott traveled to the Holy Land and brought back a bag of dirt, which he sprinkled on the graveyard. Word spread that this graveyard was a holy place, and people from all over came to be buried there. So many skeletons piled up over the centuries that they had to be moved to an ossuary to make room for others."

Skeletons again. Luis was beginning to hate the very thought of them. They'd seriously disrupted his world. Worse, they'd put terror into the heart of the woman he loved.

That thought stopped him cold.

Love was for poets. For hopeless romantics. For oversexed teenagers. What he felt for Claire…

He looked at her and his chest squeezed. In that

moment, he joined the ranks of poets. He loved this woman with all that was in him. The realization poured into every corner of his mind, so powerful that he had to struggle to take in Father Milosec's comments.

"I strongly recommend you visit this place, Dr. Cantwell, and see it for yourself. There is perhaps no more vivid manifestation of the Slavic preoccupation with death, such as his eminence described in his treatise."

"We were planning to fly home after my interview with the cardinal, but…"

Claire glanced at Luis. He could read in her face the desire to grasp at what might be their last straw.

"You say this town is only an hour away?" he asked the priest.

"Yes. I'll write the directions for you."

Another uniformed guide escorted them back to the main entrance. Claire had no idea so many people comprised the cardinal's staff, but they'd certainly impressed her with their efficiency.

Now if only she could decipher the directions Father Milosec had written out. The towns and streets all had Czech names, some of them fifteen or twenty letters long.

"Good thing our rental car comes equipped with

a Never-Lost GPS system," she muttered to Luis as they retraced their way along the catwalk that tunneled through the scaffolding. "I hope it's programmed for the areas outside Prague. If not, it'll take an hour to key in some of these names." She fished inside her purse for her cell phone. "I'd better call Major Talbot and advise her of another delay."

"Mmm."

The noncommittal reply brought her head around. Luis's gaze was trained upward at a sharp angle. Deep creases furrowed his forehead.

"What are you looking at?"

"That statue."

She craned her neck to study the large stone saint with an open book in one hand and a long staff in the other. He was only one of many lining the pediment above the palace.

"What's so interesting about that one?"

"I thought I saw a shadow behind it. Before we went into the palace. It could have been one of the workers, but…"

"Oh, dear God! It's moving. Luis! The statue's moving!"

Claire barely got the words out before the larger-than-life marble saint tipped forward. He fell off the pediment, dropped a story and hit the scaffolding, where he broke into monster chunks that plunged through the steel bars.

The bizarre incident happened in the blink of an eye. One moment, Claire was gaping at the tottering saint. The next, she put everything she had into a sideways lunge that knocked Luis off the catwalk and took her with him.

Chapter 8

The crash caused a furor.

Tourists wandering through the palace courtyard screamed and covered their heads to protect
themselves from flying debris. An elaborately uniformed guard came running from the next courtyard. The two plasterers working to restore the
window arch high up in the scaffolding almost fell
off their perch, craning to see what had happened.

Luis didn't wait for the cloud of white dust raised
by the marble chunks to settle. Rolling to his feet,
he dragged Claire up with him. "Are you hurt?"

She glanced at the shattered fragments only a
few feet away and shook her head. "No."

That's all he waited to hear. Flinging himself at the metal framework, he went up it like a jungle beast after its prey. In her slim black skirt and pumps, Claire couldn't follow. She raced back inside the palace instead.

"The roof," she shouted at the startled receptionist. "Where are the stairs to the roof?"

"What has happened?"

"A statue fell."

Or was pushed. Her jaw went tight and hard at the possibility.

"How do I get to the roof?"

The urgent demand brought the guard who'd escorted her and Luis from the cardinal's chamber running back into the reception hall. He skidded to a stop and gaped at fine white dust coating Claire's hair and skirt until her message got through to him.

"The roof? Come, it is this way."

They ran down a wide hall to a storeroom tucked into a corner tower, then up five stories of narrow, winding stairs. Panting, Claire burst onto a small wooden platform that looked over a forest of chimneys and steeply pitched eaves covered with gray slate.

A narrow walkway led to the pediment mounted above the palace's front edifice. There was no rope or railing, only six inches of naked slate slanting downward at a sharp angle.

When Claire kicked off her pumps, the guard issued an instant protest. "Madam! It is too dangerous!"

She ignored him and took the steep path, running lightly on the balls of her feet. The pediment, with its frieze of marble saints, loomed directly below. Twenty yards. Ten. Five.

She hit the bottom of the slope, breathing fast. The guard came down behind her much more slowly. There was just enough level space behind the statues for a more or less level pathway. Loose stones and bits of slate shredded the soles of Claire's panty hose as she and the guard made their cautious way to the empty spot at the center of the frieze.

They went carefully now, keeping a wary eye on several cracks in the marble pediment. They'd almost reached the center, when a scrabble of heels on stone spun Claire to the right. She ripped up the flap of her purse and was reaching for the Baretta nested inside, when she spotted Luis sliding down one of the steeply pitched eaves. His frustrated expression answered her question, but she asked it anyway.

"Nothing?"

He shook his head.

Together, they inched closer to a spot where the fallen saint had once gazed out over the palaces of the castle. All along the edge of the frieze lay bits of broken slate and loose pebbles—too loose to imprint precise footprints, although scratches and scrapes in the slate suggested some foot traffic.

Aside from those, they didn't spot any evidence someone had lurked behind the statue, waiting to send it crashing down. No cigarette butts. No discarded gum wrappers or threads caught in cracks. No chance the police could dust there for fingerprints. Too many centuries of dirt and debris. With a last look at the gaping hole once filled by the marble saint, Claire, Luis and the guard made their way back up the narrow slate pathway.

Some forty minutes later, Claire glanced around the crowded antechamber of the archbishop's palace. So far, she and Luis had provided the details of their close call to the lieutenant of the elaborately uniformed palace guards; a very concerned Father Milosec and several members of his staff; two local police officers; a detective from what was described as the Bureau of Tourist Security; and—after Luis presented his credentials to the detective—a senior rep from the Czech Republic's diplomatic service.

In the process, the near-victims had been offered a cup of soothing peppermint tea, iced orangeade and/or a bracing glass of pilsner. Luis opted for the beer. Claire went with the tea. She took a sip from her second cup as the detective approached.

"I had spoken with supervisor of work crew again," he said in labored English.

With a brusque gesture, he indicated the big, beefy craftsman who'd been summoned to account for his workmen on the scene. The man stood on the far side of the vast antechamber, flanked by two very nervous plasterers.

"He says again, only two men on job today. They are working on windows when you walk out of palace."

"I'm sure there was a third," Luis insisted.

"But you can give no description?"

"I told you. All I saw was a shadow of movement up on the pediment where the statues are mounted."

"You go up to roof," the detective reminded him patiently, "as I did. We find only scuff marks. Could be made by anyone who has come to inspect damage from earthquake last year."

"So many of the palaces in the castle complex sustained damage in that near disaster," Father Milosec put in, his face tight with concern above his black cassock. He was still visibly upset by his guests' narrow escape. "This is why you see so much restoration work in progress. The pediment was next on the list for repair. I'm sick to think we left it until almost too late." He made a heartfelt sign of the cross. "Thanks be to God you were not hurt in this accident."

Claire shared a glance with Luis. *He* obviously believed it was no accident, and she trusted his instincts. Nor could she dismiss the fact that this incident came just days after the attack outside her condo.

Coincidence? Not hardly, she thought, as Father Milosec drew a slender silver chain from the pocket of his cassock. At the end of the chain dangled an oval medal.

"I had one of my staff take this to Cardinal Tuma. He has blessed it for you."

Claire peered at the figure depicted on the medal, recognizing the open book and staff. "Isn't that the saint who crashed down on us?"

"It is. He is St. Benedict, a most holy man and the founder of the Benedictine Order. We believe his medal protects the wearer from evil. *I* believe he drew your eyes heavenward this morning, just in time to save you from death or serious injury. Please, take this and wear it with the cardinal's blessing."

"Thank you."

Claire had been raised Protestant, but she willingly bent her head so the priest could slip the chain over it. After the nightmare last night and missing death by inches this afternoon, she wouldn't refuse any good-luck talisman.

"I have one for you also, Colonel Esteban. Perhaps… Perhaps this shadow you saw was the brush of an angel's wings, alerting you to the presence of danger."

Luis accepted the medal with a murmured word of thanks and an expression Claire couldn't quite read. He held it in the palm of his hand while Father Milosec reclaimed her attention.

"The Cistercian order we spoke of earlier—the one that founded the monastery at Sedlec—it is an offshoot of the Benedictines."

Claire blinked. Good grief! Another coincidence? If so, this mission was getting extremely weird.

"Perhaps St. Benedict is adding his voice to mine," the priest said quietly. "Perhaps he, too, is telling you that you must go to Sedlec to find the weapons to fight the demons you described to the cardinal."

"We intend to go," she replied, glancing at her watch. "First thing tomorrow morning."

With the midafternoon visit to Cardinal Tuma, St. Benedict's tumble and extended sessions with various police officials, it was now past 5:00 p.m. According to Father Milosec, the drive to Sedlec was a good hour each way. And that assumed they didn't get lost on the unfamiliar roads with unpronounceable names. Claire wasn't sure how much time she'd need in the ossuary but didn't want to constrain herself by a rushed visit.

She'd already called Major Talbot to advise the pilot of yet another delay. The major hadn't sounded too disappointed at spending another night in Prague. The prospect roused mixed emotions in Claire, however. She hated the thought of Stacy Andrews suffering more nightmares while her psychologist was an ocean away, still digging for clues to the cause of her dreams.

Then there was Claire's mounting indecision regarding Luis. Cool logic argued she should stick to her insistence they take their relationship one step at a time. After last night, though, she couldn't seem to decide what that step should be. She needed to analyze her dream more dispassionately. Determine its implications. Assuage the guilt buried in the nightmare's complex layers. Yet logic seemed to be taking a backseat where Luis Esteban was concerned.

The detective broke into her thoughts with a promise and a request. "We will look on the roof again. Here is my card. You will call me and I will tell you if we find anything, yes?"

Nodding, Claire slid his card into her shoulder bag. She and Luis kept a wary eye on the pediment when they left the archbishop's palace a second time.

Fortunately, the Savoy was able to move them right back into the same suite. After the porter brought up their bags, Claire dropped into a chair and voiced the thought she knew had to be uppermost in Luis's mind as well hers.

"If that wasn't an accident—if there *was* someone on that roof—what do you think the odds are that this incident is related to the attack outside my condo?"

"Extremely high. *If* there was someone on the roof."

She nodded, her eyes grave. "I think so, too. And since the only reason for our visit to Prague is Stacy Andrews, I'm becoming convinced that both incidents are related to her nightmares."

"But how?" Luis paced the elegant suite, as tense as a coiled tiger. "I tell you, Claire, I'm not a superstitious man. One cannot be, in my business. Yet these dreams of flesh melting away. Saints falling or being pushed off their pedestal. The shadow Father Milosec attributes to angels' wings. I begin to wonder…"

He paused, started to say something, cut himself off. Frowning, he shook his head. "I begin to wonder who—or what—we're dealing with."

Her eyes widened. She wouldn't have thought he would buy into Father Milosec's theory of angels and demons. Then again, she didn't have any better theory to put forward.

"Maybe we'll find the answers in Sedlec."

"I hope so," he replied with considerable feeling.

Claire dug her cell phone out of a shoulder bag weighted with the familiar feel of her Baretta. Not that it would do her much good if they *were* battling supernatural beings.

"I need to advise Lightning of the latest developments and bring him up to speed on the results of our interview with Cardinal Tuma. I suppose I'd better contact Tom Fogarty at the White House, too."

"While you make your calls, I'll take a walk. I want to stretch my legs."

Judging by his sweat-drenched clothes after his workout at the hotel's spa earlier this morning, he'd already stretched them to the max. But Claire didn't question his decision. Like her, he was still trying to sort through everything that had happened in the past few hours and days.

"I won't be long," he told her. "Don't leave the hotel while I am gone."

"Excuse me?"

Her cool reply jerked him out of his preoccupation. One corner of his mouth curved in a rueful smile.

"*Please* do not leave the hotel." His glance dropped to the silver medal resting just above the neckline of her dirtied and torn silk blouse. "I wish I could trust St. Benedict to protect you, but…"

She didn't remind him she'd been extremely well trained to protect herself. But what good was that training against saints falling out of the sky?

The same thought swirled through Luis's mind as he wove through late-afternoon pedestrians and tourists. His route took him down winding streets to Lower Town, and then onto the Charles Bridge. The statues gazing down at him as he crossed received several scowling glances.

He'd spent most of his life in uniform, first in the ranks of Cartoza's army, then as its chief of security. By inclination and training, he was a man of action. This cat-and-mouse game with an unseen, unidentified foe was beginning to wear on his nerves. He didn't buy into the absurd notion that their foe might be some supernatural force maliciously directing events from above. Not for an instant.

Yet when he approached the bookshop where Claire had purchased her guide to the ghosts and ghouls of Prague, his brisk pace slowed. Against his better judgment, almost against his will, he reached for the door handle.

The same elderly clerk who'd assisted them yesterday was once again manning the cluttered desk that served as a counter. The tinkle of the doorbell brought his head up. Peering at Luis over his rimless glasses, he smiled a greeting.

"*Blaho odpoledne.* You come to my shop yesterday, yes? With the beautiful American lady?"

"I did."

The shopkeeper pushed away from the desk and rose. "How may I help you?"

Luis almost couldn't bring himself to voice his request. It was so ridiculous, so outside the reality he lived and worked in every day, he cringed at the mere thought of what he was about to ask. Then he remembered Claire's terrified face when he'd burst into her room last night and the words spilled from him.

"Do you have any books dealing with methods to ward off evil spirits?"

He half expected the shopkeeper to laugh in his face, or at least lift a politely derisive brow. Instead, the man nodded solemnly.

"But of course. Prague is a very old city. Many spirits walk our streets. Not all of them are benevolent."

Luis didn't really want to hear that. Still, he spent an intense half hour at the café on the next block, skimming the two volumes he'd purchased. What he read sent him on a determined search of several shops before he took the tram back up to the Savoy.

The uniformed doorman recognized him on sight. Smiling, he reached to open the ornate glass doors.

"Did you have a good walk, Colonel?"

"Very good."

"Excellent. Welcome back to…er…"

He broke off, his polite smile disintegrating as he caught a whiff of the powerful scents emanating from the plastic sack Luis gripped in one hand. The doorman shot a disbelieving glance at the bag before making a valiant attempt to recover.

"Have, uh, a good evening, sir."

"Thank you."

Luis didn't blame the man. His own eyes had been watering since his last stop at a small shop tucked away in a narrow lane in Prague's centuries-old Jewish Quarter. Feeling two parts ridiculous, one part utterly determined, he made a beeline for the elevators.

When the elevator door slid open, a couple of businessmen hurried across the lobby to get on with him. After one whiff, they took a sharp detour.

Claire's reaction mirrored theirs. She was coming out of her room when Luis entered the suite. Their paths would have crossed, if she hadn't wrinkled her nose and taken a hurried step back.

"What on earth is that stink?"

Acutely embarrassed but determined to see this through, Luis lifted the plastic bag. "Garlic, for protection against vampires. Hair of a yellow dog, to ward off werewolves. Fennel root, to keep the dead in the ground where they belong. A knotted cord soaked in white clover and urine."

Claire's jaw dropped. She gaped at him, utterly confounded for several seconds, then said faintly, "And you brought all this back with you because…?"

"For the same reason Father Milosec gave you the St. Benedict medal. To keep you safe."

Luis couldn't believe he'd actually said that, much less hunted down all these absurd talismans. Yet the mysticism he'd ruthlessly suppressed for so many years now had him by the throat. Or more correctly, by the heart. That, Luis thought wryly, was what love did to a man.

Depositing the bag on a table, he approached Claire. Enough stink came with him for her to blink several times, but she gamely stood her ground.

"My head tells me we're dealing with very human opponents, *querida*. Person or persons unknown who, for whatever reasons of their own, don't want you to uncover the cause of Stacy Andrews's nightmares. Yet, as much as I wish to, I cannot one hundred percent dismiss the ridiculous notion there may be other forces at work."

Claire bit her lip. Of all the strange and unexpected happenings that had occurred since her first call to the White House, this had to be the most bizarre!

Was this really Luis standing there, giving off such a stench? Charming, sophisticated Luis? The hardheaded colonel who believed first in the skill of his troops and second in the strength of their firepower? Had he really resorted to hunting down charms and remedies straight out of the Dark Ages?

"I know," he said with a twist of his lips. "I hear myself saying these things and can hardly believe my ears. All the while I searched for these objects, I told myself I how absurd the hunt was."

Blowing out a long breath, he cupped her chin. "My only excuse, *mi corazón,* is that I would give whatever remains of my soul to keep you safe."

Her mind whirling, Claire tried to corral her chaotic thoughts. She'd seen this man in so many different guises. The lethal, no-holds-barred operative. The ultrasuave diplomat. The incredibly skilled lover.

But she could never remember seeing him so vulnerable. In that moment, with his dark eyes holding hers and his hand ripe with an aroma that clogged her nostrils, she knew that she loved him. Wholly. Completely.

Yet…

Yet…

Her precise, logical mind refused to shut down

and surrender to emotion. An insidious whisper deep in her psyche reminded her there were no guarantees in life. Given Luis's predilection for tricky and occasionally dangerous missions on his country's behalf, he regularly put himself in the line of fire. She could lose him, too, as she'd lost Dave. Any day. Any op. This afternoon was a prime example.

Could she survive another wrenching loss? Did she want to open herself to that kind of pain again by tearing down the last barrier and laying it all out there? Her head battling fiercely with her heart, Claire took refuge behind a smile.

"No one's ever brought me fennel or a piece of urine-soaked rope before. I'd kiss you for that, but I'm afraid I might gag. Why don't you put that stuff out on the terrace and take a quick shower so I can thank you properly?"

"I have a better plan."

He retrieved the bag and deposited it outside. When he strode back into the suite, he scooped Claire up his arms.

"I'll take a very *long* shower, and you can thank me by scrubbing my back."

The hot spark in his eyes suggested he had more than back-scrubbing in mind. Claire's pulse leaped in instant response, and her belly went tight with hunger. After their near death at the castle, all thought of keeping the man at arm's length during their mission had evaporated.

"Sounds like a plan to me."

Her husky response spurred him to swift and very direct action.

A swift kick sent the bathroom door back on its hinges. With a low growl, he set her on her feet and found the clip that held her hair in its usual neat twist. His hands were rough, almost clumsy, as he released the clip, but Claire barely felt the sharp pull on her scalp.

Her pulse raced, and her hands were as clumsy as his. She had his shirt buttons undone and was attacking his belt, when he reached inside the open-stall shower and gave the control lever a swift twist. Water hissed against the glass-block wall. Before she guessed his intent, he tugged her inside fully clothed.

Laughing, she kicked off her shoes and didn't bother to protest the instant demise of her silk blouse. Especially when Luis backed her against the glass blocks. Her mouth open and greedy under his, she angled her elbows so he could peel off the wet silk. He tugged down the zipper of her slim skirt next. It slithered over her hips and landed with a plop on the tiles.

"Have I told you how beautiful you are?" he growled as he cupped her lace-covered breasts.

"Not recently."

"You, my darling, are exquisite." He bent to drop kisses on her mounded flesh. "So smooth, so warm, so delicate. Like a porcelain figurine come to life."

Claire didn't feel "smooth" or "delicate," and she'd shot past "warm" five seconds after he tugged her into the shower. She was hot for him, blazing with desire. She drew his head up, intending to smother him with kisses, but Luis preempted her.

"I meant what I said, Claire. I would give my soul to keep you safe from all harm."

"I know."

His dark eyes burned into hers. Blocking the water with his body, he propped a hand on the glass blocks behind her head. His soaked shirt molded his powerful shoulders. Rivulets ran down its open front and glistened on his bronze chest.

"Marry me, *querida*. Let me love you. Today. Tomorrow. Always."

Claire swallowed. Hard. The fierce battle between cool reason and hot emotion still raged inside her. She wasn't ready to declare a victor.

But if not now, when?

If not with Luis, then who?

There was only one answer to that. She blinked the water from her eyes, dragged in a deep breath, and crossed her own personal Rubicon.

"Yes."

His face took on a look of almost comical surprise. Silencing her inner battle once and for all, Claire smiled and framed his face with her hands.

"Yes, I'll marry you. Today. Tomorrow. Whenever you say."

She expected him to swoop in for a triumphant kiss. A savage light leaped into his eyes and she could feel the muscles quiver in the arm brushing her temple. But he exerted the iron control she so admired, and searched her face.

"Are you sure?"

"Yes," she said again, loud enough for him to hear her clearly this time.

Still, he held back. "Just yesterday you wanted to go slowly. What made you change your mind?"

"The hair of a yellow dog."

His jaw went slack, but she was too hungry for him to explain the complex rush of emotion that gripped her. All she could do was hook her arms around his neck and plaster her body against his in a kiss that rocked both their worlds.

Chapter 9

Luis woke to the sonorous bong of cathedral bells, his woman curled into his side. He lay still for a few moments, savoring the feel of her sleek body nestled against his.

In the hazy light of dawn, he couldn't quite believe he'd blurted out a proposal last night, with no romantic lead-in or finesse. Much less that Claire had really agreed to marry him! Yet she had, and Luis was damned well holding her to that reckless promise—as he proceeded to inform her some moments later when her lids fluttered up.

Propping himself up on one elbow, he brushed

a strand of pale gold hair from her cheek. "Good morning, *mi esposa.*"

The endearment produced a startled look, but she recovered with a smile. "Good morning."

"So, what are your thoughts on where and when we shall have our wedding?"

"We kept kind of busy last night. I haven't had time to think where and when."

"Think now."

"Can I go to the bathroom before we get into any heavy discussions?" she asked dryly.

"As long as you come back to me." He patted the mattress. "Here."

Sleep had coated Claire's teeth with fuzz and her body still felt the aftereffects of a long night of love, but the unmistakable invitation in his eyes gave her sluggish pulse a decided kick. It accelerated several notches during the short trip to the bathroom, only to hit a speed bump when she faced herself in the mirror above the marble sink.

"Dear God! What have I done?"

A flutter of sheer panic rippled along her spine. She suppressed the shudder almost as soon as it hit. She knew exactly what she'd done. She'd agreed to marry the man who refused to let her keep him at arm's length any longer.

The rationale for her decision came easy this morning. She'd been an observer for too long now.

Too content to listen to other people's doubts and fears. Too ready to sublimate her own needs in her practice, with the occasional adrenaline spike of her missions for OMEGA.

"It's time to get back in the game," she told the tousle-haired woman in the mirror. "Past time!"

And Luis was just the man to do it with. He challenged her. Aroused her. Irritated her immensely at times. But always, *always,* intrigued her.

Gripped by a suddenly overwhelming impatience to get back to him, she splashed water on her face and grabbed her toothbrush. Mere moments later, she slid between the sheets. He welcomed her with an arm curled around her shoulders.

"Are you ready to discuss arrangements now?"

"Actually," she countered, skimming her nails over the hair dusting his naked chest, "I have something else in mind at the moment."

He lifted a brow but didn't argue. Relaxing against the pillows, he let her explore the planes and ridges of his upper torso. His loose sprawl tightened considerably when Claire ran her palm over his belly.

The hair at his groin was thicker, stiffer. She used her nails again, lightly, teasingly, and smiled when he jerked to life under her fingertips. Her breath catching on a rush of pure desire, she cupped his sac.

* * *

Claire emerged from the bathroom for the second time thirty minutes later. Showered, shampooed and dressed in gray slacks and her lemon-colored tank top, she had already shifted mental gears to the task ahead.

"We have to hustle," she warned, skimming a glance down his length. Hard to believe what the man could do to jeans and an open-neck white shirt with the cuffs rolled up! "Major Talbot said we need to take off by two p.m., or she'd have to request a crew waiver."

"We'll make it. But first…"

Before Claire understood his intent, he retrieved the plastic shopping bag he'd left out on the terrace overnight. The ripe odor had subsided somewhat, but still carried a punch.

"Luis! You don't seriously intend to bring that stuff with us?"

"It does us no good here."

She started to protest that his aromatic home remedies were based on pure superstition. The silver chain and small, oval St. Benedict medal she'd slipped on while dressing blunted that argument.

Saints and angels. Devils and demons. People had believed in both for centuries. Still believed, Claire admitted with a shiver as Luis dropped the plastic sack in a large container with a press-down lid.

"I had room service deliver this. They swear it is airtight. It will contain the smell."

"It better, or we'll get some *very* strange looks when we arrive at Sedlec."

"Let me see the directions again."

Side by side, they studied the handwritten instructions and accompanying map.

"Sedlec is a suburb of Kutná Hora." Claire tapped the *X* denoting their destination. "It looks like a fair-size town. We should be able to follow the signs and go right to it."

Should, being the operative word, she was forced to admit almost two hours later.

By mutual agreement, Luis drove while Claire navigated. They'd spent the first portion of the trip in the discussion they'd postponed earlier. She brightened Luis's day considerably by telling him she didn't want a big, splashy wedding. She'd gone that route once and would always hold the memory in her heart. This time around, she didn't need a lot of pomp and show—only the presence of their friends at a small ceremony, followed by a reception dinner at their favorite restaurant.

"My staff will take care of everything," he promised.

Living arrangements were next on the list of topics. That negotiation carried them through

Prague's suburbs. Luis agreed they should make Claire's condo their primary residence and use his ambassadorial quarters for official functions.

Also high on the list of topics was how they'd manage their separate careers once he completed his stint as Cartoza's ambassador to the United States. That particular discussion lasted until they exited the main road and hit the Central Bohemian countryside.

Any other time, Claire would have admired the rich, rolling farmlands and picturesque villages. If not for the omnipresent satellite dishes, the stone houses with their slate roofs and chickens pecking in the front yards might have come right out of the Middle Ages. Unfortunately, few of the signposts leading to these villages matched the spelling on Father Milosec's instructions. Two or three turns, and they were hopelessly lost.

At that point, Claire was forced to do battle with the rental car's dubiously named Never-Lost system. Obviously, its computer had been programmed for Prague's immediate environs. When she tried to key in some of the towns from Father Milosec's instructions, the system didn't recognize them. She tried five or six different spellings of Kutná Hora before the computer finally translated one to the Czech name, Hory Kutné.

Even when they finally reached the city itself,

they weren't home free. As Luis had indicated, it was a large city. A sign on the outskirts indicated its town center had been designated a UNESCO World Heritage Site. Claire caught only a few lines of the English inscribed on the sign.

"It says Kutná Hora owes its origin to the silver mines in this area," she read, twisting around in her seat to read the rest. "King Wenceslas II issued some kind of decree in thirteen hundred to govern the mines' operations and ordered the construction of the Cathedral of St. Barbara in thanks for their riches."

A truck rattled by, obscuring the rest of the sign, and Claire settled back in her seat. She could see the magnificent Gothic cathedral rising above the city directly ahead. Its multiple spires speared into an achingly blue sky. Their lacy stonework formed a tribute to both the glory of God and the immense wealth of the region.

Too bad the spires proved totally worthless as navigational beacons. Within moments of entering Kutná Hora's narrow, twisting streets, Claire and Luis were lost. The construction barriers erected at almost every turn in the town's historic center didn't help matters. Luis pulled over twice so Claire could ask directions, but neither of the people they stopped could speak English.

After driving down several blind alleys, Luis

finally pulled up at a small tobacco shop/convenience store. The interior was dark and smoky, and the three locals hunched around a dime-size table eyed the newcomers curiously. Claire smiled a greeting, or started to. Her smile slipped when she noted their boots, baggy trousers and loose-fitting shirts.

These men looked eerily like the farmers in her and Stacy Andrews's nightmare!

Her breath caught. Her heart started to pound. Shaken, she glanced around. She half expected to spot a wooden pitchfork or scythe leaning up against a wall. To her immense relief, her gaze took in only racks of magazines, an array of tobacco products, shelves crammed with canned goods and several strings of sausages hanging above the counter where Luis had spread their map.

"Sedlec?"

The burly shopkeeper eyed the spot he pointed to and nodded vigorously. *"Ano, Sedlec."*

"Where? What direction?"

"Ano, ano." The man thumbed the countertop several times. "Sedlec."

Luis turned to Claire. "I think he means we're here."

"I think so," she agreed, still tingling from the odd sensation of a moment ago. "Church of All Saints?" she tried. "Ossuary?"

"Ahhh!" Enlightenment dawned. Coming out from behind the counter, the shopkeeper gestured for them to follow him to the door. Once out on the stoop, he pointed to a slender spire just visible over the slate rooftops.

"*Kostnice.* Ossuary."

"Thank you!"

They reached the church a few moments later and parked behind several other vehicles with rental car plates. As difficult as it was to find, the site obviously drew its share of tourists.

Claire climbed out and slung the strap of her purse over her shoulder. While Luis keyed the car lock, she studied the baroque facade of the church. It didn't compare to the cathedrals of Prague and Kutná Hora in either size or magnificence. This was a parish church, designed and built to serve the needs of a small community.

As was the cemetery adjoining the church. Enclosed by the stone wall, it held at most forty or fifty graves. Some of the headstones marking those graves were new, shiny marble freshly inscribed with names and dates. Time had weathered others so badly their lettering was indecipherable. Hard to believe this tree-shaded patch of ground had served as the burial place for thousands over the centuries.

Claire didn't appreciate how *many* thousands

until they followed the path that led to the entrance to the underground bone repository. The sign posted outside the entrance contained information in Czech, English and German. As Father Milosec had indicated, the present church had been built on the site of an eleventh-century Cistercian monastery. The ossuary came later, after the cemetery gained fame as a holy place.

"Good Lord!" Claire gasped. "It says here that somewhere between forty to seventy thousand people were buried here over the centuries."

The rest of the information was almost as startling. The present two-story church had been constructed in the early 1400s, with a vaulted upper level, and a chapel on the lower level to store skeletons dug up to make room for new burials. For centuries, bones had stacked up in the lower chamber. Then, in 1870, the duke who ruled this region commissioned a wood-carver to put the bones in order.

"'His efforts are as artistic as they are startling,'" Claire read aloud.

Goose bumps rose on her arms. She didn't have a good feeling about this. Her unease grew as they approached the entrance. Two steps later, she stopped dead.

A ticket taker sat in a dusty glass booth just inside the entrance. The arch above the ticket booth was studded with skulls and crossed femurs.

That alone was enough to send a shiver down Claire's spine, but it was the massive arrangement on the opposite wall that held her astonished gaze. More skulls, femurs and scapulars had been fashioned into the universal symbol of the Catholic Church—the letters IHE—topped by a bone cross, and what was obviously intended as rays emanating outward. Claire swallowed hard, staring in unwilling fascination at the macabre arrangement, while Luis purchased entry tickets.

"Two, please."

The cheerful, red-cheeked attendant took the bill he slid toward her and returned his change, along with a thin brochure.

"You want in English, yes?"

"Yes."

She glanced from Luis to Claire and back again. "You come from America?"

"My friend does."

"I haf visited my cousin Magda in a place called Oklahoma. Her city is called Prague, like our own city. You know this place?"

"Sorry, I don't."

"It is very small, this Prague, but many Czechs live there." Smiling, she gestured to a leather-bound book. "Please to sign our guest register."

Luis complied, and the woman slid two tissue-thin tickets through the window.

"Please to enjoy our ossuary."

Enjoy was *not* the verb Claire would use in association with the feelings that crawled over her as she and Luis descended the shallow steps. Before entering the chapel itself, they came face-to-face with a windowed niche containing hundreds of skulls piled in neat rows, one on top of the other. A flickering candle illuminated the coins left in a tray in front of the window.

"Offerings to the dead," Luis murmured, adding a handful of change to the pile.

Claire had no desire to contribute to the offerings. Her throat felt tight. A fine film of sweat had dampened her palms. Wrenching her gaze from the rows of empty, sightless sockets, she stepped down into the chapel itself and immediately wished she hadn't.

Bones and skulls decorated almost every square inch of the sanctuary. On the walls, on the staves of the vaulted ceiling, on every door and window frame. Even the seven-foot-tall candelabra beside the altar was topped by angelic cherubs who didn't appear the least bit disturbed at being entwined for all eternity with human remains.

Dominating all, however, was the massive chandelier hanging in the center of the chapel. Her palms clammy, Claire had to fight the urge to back away from the bones that dangled from its lower branches like the tinkling crystal drops on a Waterford chandelier. She sure as hell wasn't about to have her picture taken directly under the thing, like the young woman toting a heavy backpack, who struck a pose for her equally encumbered friend.

"The brochure says the chandelier contains at least one of every bone in the human body," Luis read quietly.

Claire tried to tell herself this was a unique form of art. That the woodcutter who arranged these skeletal remains had intended to inspire awe and reverence for the dead. But none of the arguments she struggled to marshal could combat the icy sensations rippling down her spine.

She felt as though she was living her nightmare. They crowded her, all these skulls and skeletal remains. Smothered her. She couldn't breathe, couldn't think.

"Look at the royal insignia," Luis said, completely absorbed by the monstrous coat of arms depicted in human remains. "Is that a raven pecking at the eye socket of that skull?"

She gave a strangled gasp. "I need some air. Now!"

Smothering an oath, he grasped her elbow and steered her to the short flight of steps. She lurched up the steps, barely able to breathe. Their precipitous exit drew a startled glance from the ticket seller.

"Madam?" She jumped up and grabbed one of the bottles of water for sale in the booth.

Claire didn't stop for the bottle the woman thrust through the ticket window. She had to get out in the sunshine, had to banish the images that pecked at the edges of her sanity like the raven Luis had pointed to.

She made it as far as the low stone wall before her legs collapsed. She sank onto the ledge and dragged in air. Bit by bit, the dark images receded and were replaced by Luis's handsome, worried face.

"Forgive me, my darling. I was so mesmerized by that place, I did not see how it affected you. Are you all right?"

"Now."

"Here, madam." The ticket seller hurried over to them with the plastic bottle clutched in her hand. "Drink. The water is from the stream behind the church. It is blessed and will banish the ghosts."

Claire wasn't about to gulp down water from a stream that filtered through a cemetery.

"Thank you, but I'm fine now. I just needed some air."

"Our ossuary does this to some," the woman admitted apologetically. "Even big men, strong men, grow faint."

Still trying to steady her breathing, Claire merely

nodded. The woman's next comment snared her full attention, however.

"One of your countrymen was similarly taken just weeks ago. His face was ashen, but he asks many questions, makes many notes. He wants, too, to see our parish records from many years ago. I think he looks for his ancestors, but he shakes his head when I ask this."

Luis's glance locked with Claire's. She guessed instantly what he was thinking. Another coincidence?

"Did this man sign the guest register?" he wanted to know.

"He does not, but the one with him does."

"May I see the entry?"

"*Ano.* Come, I will show you."

"Don't move," he instructed Claire. "I'll be right back."

Feeling more revived by the moment, Claire let the strap of her shoulder bag slip down her arm and rested her palms on the stone ledge. Bit by bit, the quiet tranquility soothed her jagged nerves. Sunlight dappled through the trees shading the cemetery. Honeysuckle spilled over one corner of the wall and filled the air with its perfumed scent.

Her gaze strayed to a rusted iron cross tilting against the wall, mere inches from the bright yellow blossoms.

Was there something in this tranquil setting that might help Stacy Andrews? Or something Claire had missed inside the ossuary? Those cherubs topping the gruesome candelabra? The creepy chandelier? They *could* be interpreted as shedding light after death.

She was still trying to put a positive spin on the artwork inside the ossuary when a shadow of movement near its entrance caught her eye.

Her pulse skipped a beat. Angels' wings? Again?

Not this time.

This time it was Luis who emerged from the shadows. Claire watched him stride toward her, so tall, so confident, so damned handsome, and a sense of absolute rightness settled around her heart.

Chapter 10

Claire called into OMEGA's control center during the drive back to Prague. It was still early in the States, not yet 4:00 a.m., but her controller was at the desk.

No surprise there. When Joe Devlin acted as controller for an agent in the field, he pulled round-the-clock duty. Claire would do the same for any operative she controlled.

"Yo, Cyrene." Rigger's lazy Oklahoma drawl came through the earpiece. "You and El Colonél on your way home?"

"Almost."

"How was the visit to Sedlec?"

"Creepy, but productive. We may have something."

Or nothing. So two American men had rooted around in parish records some weeks ago? Claire had no proof they'd been looking for information about Stacy Andrews's great-grandfather. Or that they were in any way connected to falling statues or presently deceased muggers.

"I need you to check someone out, Rigger."

"Can do easy."

She heard the sound of a thump. The back legs of his chair hitting the floor, she guessed.

"Shoot."

"His name is Alex Dawson. He signed the guest register at the Sedlec ossuary on April twentieth and gave his home as Richmond, Virginia."

"Alex Dawson. Richmond. Got it."

"See if you can make any link between this guy Dawson and the man who attacked us outside my condo."

"Edward Porter? Will do."

"Also…"

"Yeah?"

"You might also run a screen of White House personnel. See if Dawson pops up in anyone's list of contacts."

It was a long shot, but Claire was fast running out of options. She'd hoped the bone ossuary would yield concrete clues to the root cause of Stacy Andrews's nightmares. All she'd come away with was a *much* keener appreciation of how deeply spectral remains were imbued in Bohemian history and culture.

"If there's a connection," Rigger predicted confidently, "I'll find it."

Claire signed off and tucked her phone back in its special pocket in her shoulder bag.

"Rigger's going to work it," she confirmed to Luis. "I hope he finds something. I hate going back to the president and Stacy Andrews empty-handed."

He gave her a quick glance from behind his mirrored sunglasses. They'd left the windows open to the warm spring air. The rush of wind ruffled his glossy black hair and tugged at the open neck of his shirt.

"We are hardly going back empty-handed, *querida*. We've learned much during this trip."

"All we've learned is that Stacy's great-grandfather did in fact emigrate from Bohemia."

"And that he was born in a village one might describe as the bone capital of Europe."

"So the ossuary got to you, too?"

"How could it not?" His silky black mustache twitched. "I don't believe I have ever seen skulls so artfully arranged."

Claire smiled, but had to repress an involuntary

shudder. She suspected it would take some time for the memory of those disturbing candelabra and altar decorations to fade.

"Let's not forget the matter of that statue of St. Benedict," Luis reminded her, turning serious. "I'm still not convinced its fall was an accident."

She wasn't, either, but they'd found no evidence to the contrary. A little self-consciously, she fingered the silver chain looped around her neck.

"If that wasn't an accident," she said slowly, "if someone deliberately tried to harm us, the attempt has to be linked to this visit to Prague and to Stacy Andrews's nightmares. But how? Why?"

Frustration ate at her as she came full circle.

"The only concrete facts we've uncovered here in the Czech Republic suggest Stacy's nightmares are genetic. If so, that will make her treatment more difficult and prolonged."

Claire would have to locate a specialist with more expertise in genetic predisposition for dreams than the colleagues she'd consulted so far. *If* such a specialist existed. The science was still new and pretty far out there.

"Or you could try some of the remedies I procured for you on Stacy Andrews," Luis said casually.

The suggestion produced an instant groan. "Oh no! Promise me you will *not* bring that stuff aboard the aircraft."

His noncommittal shrug left the issue unresolved.

"Luis, be serious! You can't really think I'm going to march into the White House with a sackful of fennel root and the hair of a yellow dog."

"Why not, if they work?"

"We have no evidence they do."

"I beg to differ. You didn't have nightmares last night, did you?"

That took the heat from Claire's argument. She *hadn't* dreamed last night. Luis had kept her too busy—and too exhausted!—with his hands and mouth and hard, driving body.

Then, of course, there was the marriage proposal he'd dropped on her. That had crowded almost everything else from her conscious mind. She suspected her subconscious was still trying to deal with it. How else to explain the doubts that surfaced briefly this morning, when she'd faced herself in the bathroom mirror?

Doubts she now had to struggle to recall. She'd grown more sure of her decision with each passing hour, she realized as they hit the outskirts of Prague.

Claire enjoyed a last view of the castle and magnificent cathedral dominating the city skyline before they took the bypass to the airport.

They turned in the rental car and hopped a tram to the main commercial terminal. After going through airport security and verifying their credentials, they were ferried to the auxiliary airport hangars across the runway from the main terminal. Various smaller aircraft sat outside the hangars, including the twin-engine Gulfstream with its distinctive USAF markings.

Major Talbot had indicated she'd have the jet preflighted and ready to go. But when security dropped Claire and Luis off beside the transport, they were greeted by a clearly frustrated pilot and crew.

"Sorry, ma'am. We've hit a glitch."

While the crew chief relieved Luis of the bags, the honey-haired major gestured to the hangar behind her.

"The auxiliary airport manager called down a few minutes ago. He's holding up our clearance to depart."

"Why?"

"He said something about an accident at St. Vitus Cathedral yesterday."

"What's that got to do with our departure?"

"Evidently, a representative from Bureau of Tourist Affairs just showed up at the airport. He needs you and Colonel Esteban to sign a release of liability."

"You're kidding."

"No, ma'am."

Claire curbed her impatience with this example

of bureaucratese. In a country as dependent on tourism as the Czech Republic, she supposed the government wanted assurance she wouldn't hit them with a million-dollar lawsuit and all its attendant bad press.

"The airport manager requested you stop by his office," Major Talbot said. "He'll have the release there."

"Very well." Claire passed her briefcase to the crew chief and hitched the strap of her bag higher on her shoulder. "Where's his office?"

The major hooked a thumb at the hangar that served as the Fixed Base Operations Center. "Inside, top of the stairs, fourth door to the right."

She and Luis started for the hangar. The sharp scents of a busy airport followed them. Diesel fumes from the refueling trucks outside mingled with the industrial-strength cleaner used to scrub hangar floors in an effort to keep them free of foreign objects that might be ingested into jet engines.

Judging by the rickety metal stairs leading to the offices suspended above the hangar floor, the facilities on this side of the airport were considerably older than those in the big, bright main terminal. The stairs led to a narrow corridor illuminated by bulbs hanging at the end of their cords. Several of the bulbs had burnt out and needed replacing. Their absence left large sections of the hall in deep shadow.

Luis's cell phone rang just as they started down the corridor. Frowning, he tipped the phone back toward the light to see the digital display.

"It is the Cartozan embassy here in Prague," he told Claire. "I should take this."

"Go ahead. I'll find the airport manager."

Claire counted down the doors and twisted the knob for the fourth on the right. It opened onto a small, dusty, unbelievably cluttered outer office. Aviation charts covered every available horizontal surface. Clipboards hung haphazardly from pegs. A monitor displaying weather data flickered from its perch high atop a row of metal file cabinets.

"Hello?"

A male voice responded from the inner office. "Yes?"

Claire edged past the precariously stacked charts. From what she could see of the second office, it contained as much clutter as the first. It also, she saw when she stepped through the door, contained a corpse.

The body lay sprawled on the floor, out of sight from the other office, but unavoidable once inside. It was a male, she noted in a single, searing instant. Mid to late forties. With tobacco-yellowed lips, a purple birthmark on one cheek and a neat hole in the center of his forehead.

Her veins icing, Claire made a slow quarter

turn. A second male lounged in a tipped-back chair behind a dented metal desk. His eyes were as steady and unswerving as the silenced semi-automatic aimed at her heart.

"You've led us quite a chase, Dr. Cantwell."

Before he'd even opened his mouth, Claire had switched into operative mode. In the blink of an eye, she'd assessed the man—American, late thirties, a good twenty pounds overweight. His weapon, a polycast Walther P-22 with a Gem-Tech suppressor screwed onto the muzzle.

"Us?" she echoed coolly as she made a show of clenching her fist around the strap of her shoulder bag. In the process, she slid her hand a surreptitious inch or two lower on the strap. "Who is 'us'?"

Her best option—her *only* option—at this point was to keep him talking until she could make her move. Claire's extensive research into the criminal mind supported what most street cops knew from experience. Vicious killers such as this one liked to brag about their crimes. Show how much smarter they were than their victims or the police.

With consummate skill, she managed to project the image of a woman stonily refusing to show how terrified she was while clutching her bag in a shaking, white-knuckled fist. Her hand was only inches from the purse's flap when the man on the other side of the desk pursed his fleshy lips.

"Haven't you figured it out yet? And you, with all those degrees hanging on your wall."

"Why don't you enlighten me, Mr. Dawson?"

Her guess hit home.

"That's one of the names I use," he admitted, his face tightening. "How did you make me?"

"You signed the register at the ossuary in Sedlec."

"Crap! So that's where you went." Disgust rippled across his fleshy features. "I tried to tail you when you left the hotel this morning, but lost you in traffic. Had to hang around here at the airport for hours waiting for you to show."

"Which gave you plenty of time to concoct a story about needing me to sign some kind of release and have the auxiliary field manager relay it to my crew."

"It worked, didn't it?"

All too well, Claire admitted silently. She speared a glance at the body on the floor while Dawson's gaze swept to the open door behind her.

"Where's your lover?"

Before she could respond, her cell phone pinged inside her purse. "That's probably him now," she lied.

Luis wouldn't call when he was only steps behind her. She knew that, but Dawson didn't. She guessed he wouldn't let her answer the call, but used the moment to release her death grip on the shoulder strap and move her hand toward the flap.

"Leave it!" Dawson snapped. "I need him to come looking for you."

They faced each other across the desk while the phone rang a second time. A third. After the fourth, it fell silent. Claire broke the stillness that followed with a terse question.

"Who hired you?"

"Wouldn't you like to know?" he sneered.

Claire's lips curled. She was fast developing a severe dislike for the man but had to keep him talking until she could get her hand inside her bag.

"Tell me one thing. Was that you yesterday on the roof of the archbishop's palace?"

"Yeah, it was." Malicious amusement tinged his pale blue eyes. "I couldn't believe you leaped like a damned cat out from under that statue. Just like you escaped Eddie. You're a little too quick for us, Doc. Too damned slippery. That's why we had to give up trying to make this look like an accident."

The pseudoamusement left his eyes. Claire's throat closed as they went flat and cold.

"I owe you for Eddie, Doc."

"I assume you're referring to Ed Porter, the man who attacked me outside my home."

"Yeah, bitch, I am. You crushed his windpipe. You and your greaseball lover. I intend to take care of him, too, as soon as he shows his face."

Almost before he'd mouthed the words, footsteps sounded in the corridor. That was Luis. Claire knew it. The fat pig across from her knew it.

Instinctively, his glance swung toward the office door. His gun barrel followed. It moved only an inch. Two at the most. Claire knew that was all she'd get.

"Luis!" she screamed, whipping up the flap of her purse as she flung herself to the side. "Down!"

Her hand closed around the butt of her Baretta. Her thumb hit the safety. She fired through the leather bag at the same instant her assailant's weapon kicked.

Her shot caught the beefy triggerman square in the chest and sent his chair crashing back against the wall. His, Claire saw on a shaft of sheer terror, caught the figure in the outer doorway and spun him around. Staggering, he went down on one knee.

Claire leaped around the desk and took only enough time to make sure the threat had been neutralized before rushing to Luis. He had a hand pressed against his side. Blood stained his white shirt and dripped through his fingers onto the office floor.

"The embassy...got word," he got out through clenched teeth. "OMEGA and...Interpol ID'ed... Dawson. He's...here in Prague."

"I know. That's him with his lungs decorating the wall."

Luis grunted and Claire skimmed a frantic glance

around the office for something to stanch the blood. A windbreaker hung from a wooden coatrack in a corner. She leaped up and snatched it off the rack. Folding it into a thick pad, she eased it under Luis's blood-soaked palm.

"You'll have to hold it. Just for a minute, while I call for help."

As it turned out, she didn't have to call. Dawson's weapon had been silenced, but hers wasn't. The shot brought all kinds of folks running.

The first was a young woman in jeans and a faded blue T-shirt advertising a Czech airline. When she rushed into the office and spotted Claire on her knees beside Luis, she choked out a strangled gasp.

"Call an ambulance!" Claire implored.

Either she didn't understand English or the bodies sprawled on the floor scared the crap out of her. She took off, shouting at the top of her lungs.

Her screams brought two mechanics in grease-stained overalls. They peered cautiously through the door of the outer office. When they spotted the corpse of the man she assumed was the airport manager, she thought for a moment they were going to take off shouting, too.

"Call an ambulance," she ordered, fighting to sound cool and authoritative.

It didn't help that her voice cracked on the last

word. Or that Luis had now crumpled against the file cabinets. Her heart pumping pure terror, she was reduced to begging.

"*Please!* Doctor. Medico. *Please!*"

She almost sobbed with relief when Major Talbot and her crew chief pushed past the mechanics.

"What the hell?"

"Veronica! Get a medical team here. Now!"

Goggle-eyed, the major whipped her cell phone from the pocket of her flight suit. While she struggled to relay the urgent request, her crew chief knelt beside Claire to help hold the wadded and blood-soaked windbreaker against Luis's side.

A black-suited SWAT team burst into the office mere moments later. Only after they'd secured all weapons and judged the situation safe, did they allow in the medical response team. The helmeted and heavily armed SWAT members watched closely as two EMTs edged Claire away from the now unconscious Luis.

It felt like hours, but probably took less than ten minutes, before they'd packed his wound, hooked up an IV and had him on a gurney. Claire tried to follow when they wheeled him out but wasn't surprised when the SWAT team leader detained her.

"You must give statement."

She threw an urgent look at Major Talbot. The pilot interpreted it with no difficulty.

"I'll go with him."

"Call me if—" Claire swallowed, hard, and amended her plea "—when you get to the hospital."

"I will," the major promised.

Claire spent the next thirty minutes alternating between teeth-grinding frustration and gut-wrenching terror.

She couldn't lose Luis, too!

She *couldn't!*

Sick fear curled in her belly as she struggled to overcome the language barrier. Using gestures and short, succinct phrasing, she tried to describe the sequence of events to a patently suspicious team of investigators. Belatedly, she remembered the card she'd slipped in her purse yesterday.

At her urgent request, the officer on the scene called the detective who'd investigated the incident at the cathedral. He confirmed that Dr. Cantwell had indeed been the victim of what now must be viewed as a deliberate attack. Given the physical evidence they described in this one, he felt sure she'd been defending herself against a second attack.

But it took a call to OMEGA to effect her release. Lightning himself appeared on the cell phone screen for a very direct, very emphatic conference call.

"Call Henri Celusniak, director of your country's Interpol division," Lightning instructed the Czech investigaotrs. "He'll confirm this man Dawson, aka Winston Rutherford aka Harold Popejoy, tops Interpol's list of suspected hit men."

Mere moments later, Claire raced down the metal stairs. One of the responding officers directed her to his parked vehicle. Once she was strapped in, he put the vehicle in gear and peeled away from the hangar. All the way to the hospital, one thought kept hammering at Claire's frantic mind: she told Luis she would marry him, but she'd never told him she loved him.

Chapter 11

When Claire rushed into the hospital in one of Prague's modern suburbs, she learned Luis was undergoing emergency surgery. The fear that had held her in its paralyzing grip during the way in dug deeper and twisted her insides.

Claire found Veronica Talbot in the surgical waiting area. True to her word, the pilot had stayed with Luis right up to the moment he'd been wheeled into the operating room.

"The good news is that the bullet ricocheted off a rib and exited," she related. "The bad news… The rib splintered and a shard of bone perforated his left lung."

"Did the lung collapse?"

"I'm not sure."

She hesitated, and Claire felt the air squeeze out of her own lungs.

"He lost a lot of blood. The docs didn't come right out and say so, but I got the impression it could be touch and go."

After calling her crew to give them an update, the major stuck with Claire during the tense hours that followed. It was mid-afternoon before Luis was out of surgery and moved to the ICU. Claire was there when they wheeled him in. She had to bite her lip until she tasted blood at seeing him so pale and still.

The staff was briskly efficient as they hooked him to a heart monitor and IV drips. Claire held his hand in a gentle grip until a male nurse rolled in a cart.

"Excuse, madam. I must work here. You will wait in the lounge?"

She understood the rationale for restricting visitors to ten minutes each hour, on the hour. The ICU cubicles weren't designed for family confabs and gatherings. Besides which, Luis would be out for hours. Reluctantly, she relinquished her place at his beside. She knew he couldn't hear her but leaned over to murmur to him anyway.

"I'll be right outside."

Veronica Talbot had waited in the family lounge for an update. "He okay?"

"As best I can understand, his condition is guarded."

The pilot nodded, her face grave above her flight suit. "I called in to my scheduler. Since you're staying with the ambassador and he can't be moved for an indeterminate time, they've tagged us to return to the States. They'll send another crew whenever you say the word, ma'am."

"Thanks."

"I had your luggage delivered." She gestured to the bags sitting beside one of the sofas and hesitated. "I hate to leave you here alone."

"I'll be all right. So will Luis." Claire gripped the major's hand and worked up a smile. "I know an agency in Washington that could use someone with your cool head and leadership skills. If you ever decide to leave the air force, call me."

"I will."

After the pilot departed, Claire went to the ladies' room to scrub the blood off her hands and make a quick change, then she called in an update on Luis's condition to OMEGA. Rigger, in turn, fed her the information he'd dug up on Dawson through his contacts in Interpol and British intelligence.

"He served in the British army during the first Gulf War, went mercenary in the second. That's where he hooked up with his pal Porter. The two of them hired out as personal bodyguards for a top-level Iraqi, but word on the street is they used an attack on their client to form their own private death squad."

"Bastards," Claire muttered, remembering the sadistic enjoyment Dawson had taken in taunting her.

"And then some," Rigger agreed. "They reportedly made a bundle in Iraq, then dropped off the radar screen three years ago. Interpol's tracking at least five unsolved murders they think these two had a hand in."

"What about links to the White House?"

"All we have so far are airport surveillance tapes that confirm Porter and Dawson did, in fact, fly into Prague in March, and your report that they rooted around in the parish records at Sedlec, where Stacy Andrews's great-grandfather emigrated from."

It was a tenuous connection at best, but Rigger promised to keep digging. He also promised to relay the update on Luis's condition to the Cartozan Embassy in D.C.

Claire knew the embassy would notify both Luis's brother and the president of Cartoza, as well as that country's ambassador to the Czech Republic. So she wasn't surprised when Luis's counterpart made a personal visit to the ICU to check on his fellow countryman. While there, he put his entire staff at her disposal should she or Luis need anything.

"Anything at all," he reiterated, pressing her hand between both of his own.

With his full head of gray hair and regal bearing, Diego Delgado exuded the same charm and sophistication that characterized Luis. And, as he confided to Claire, he'd once served as the colonel's superior officer.

"He is like a panther, that one. Even in darkest jungles, he moves with such speed and confidence. Has he told you of the multinational raid he led against the Norte del Valle cartel in Colombia?"

"No, he hasn't."

"Then I shall."

The telling lasted for some time. Claire suspected the ambassador omitted the more gory details but was grateful to him for helping pass the hour between allowed visits to Luis's bedside.

He accompanied her into the ICU for the next ten-minute visit. The sight of Luis hooked up to so many tubes and machines left Claire tight-chested and the ambassador looking grave. He departed soon afterward, with a promise to return in the morning.

Two detectives from Prague's homicide division showed up next. Claire spent another hour answering their questions, or trying to. She was between visits to the ICU when yet another visitor entered the waiting area. Father Milosec's cassock swirled about his ankles as he hurried over.

"Cardinal Tuma sends me with his prayers and his hopes for the colonel's swift recovery. My prayers join his."

"Thank you."

"How does he progress?"

"He lost a lot of blood." Claire scrubbed her forehead with the heel of her hand. "All the nurses will say when I ask is that his condition is guarded. I'm beginning to think that's the only English medical term they know."

"I will inquire for you, yes?"

"Yes, please."

He returned some moments later with a different spin on the same report. "They say it is in God's hands."

He spotted the small kitchenette tucked in a corner of the waiting room and poured cups of coffee for both of them before settling beside Claire on the soft-cushioned sofa.

"The police say this man who shoots the colonel also pushes over the statue of St. Benedict. Can you tell me why he does these things?"

Claire glanced around the waiting area. Only one other group was present, all huddled around their red-eyed and grieving grandfather. She doubted any of them could hear. Still, she lowered her voice.

"We don't have hard proof, but we believe those

attacks, and one that occurred back in the States, were intended to prevent me from discovering the cause of the nightmares President Andrews's daughter has experienced."

Shock rippled across the priest's face. "But why?"

Most likely, she was now convinced, to force the popular president out of office. Andrews would resign in a heartbeat to protect his daughter's health or safety. Claire kept that supposition to herself, however, and stuck to the facts.

"That's the million-dollar question. All we know for sure at this point is the man I shot made a visit to the Sedlec bone ossuary in March and asked to see the same parish records you pulled up on the computer for me."

The priest shook his head over the strangeness of it all. "What can we—Cardinal Tuma and I— do to help?"

She let out a sigh. "I don't know at this point, except perhaps to keep the prayers flowing for Luis."

"But of course. And for you, my daughter. And for you."

She didn't need prayer as much as Luis. That became ominously apparent as evening gave way to night, and night to the dark hours before dawn.

Father Milosec had offered to stay with her but she knew the frail Cardinal Tuma needed him, too. The priest left, promising to return in the morning, as had Ambassador Delgado. So it was just Claire and the family clustered around their stoop-shouldered, red-eyed grandfather all through the long night.

And the intensive care unit staff, of course. They were as sympathetic as they were efficient, but nothing could soften the sterile starkness of their unit. Monitors beeped with quiet relentlessness. Curtains rattled on their steel bearings between the units. Soft-soled shoes made squeaking noises on scrubbed tile floors. And each ten-minute visit to Luis's bedside left Claire more frightened.

This was worse, so much worse, than what she'd experienced with Dave. That awful tragedy had happened a continent away. She'd been fed only bits of information during the scant few days her husband had been held hostage. Word of the bungled rescue attempt and Dave's death had come like a slashing cut straight to her heart.

This time she was right there, leaning close to Luis during her visits to his bedside, threading her fingers through his, murmuring his name. He drifted in and out during those visits. Even during his "in" moments, he was so doped up she knew nothing really registered.

Only once did he seem to respond to the sound of her voice. His eyelids twitched and his fingers seemed to tighten in hers. She leaned closer, her heart thumping.

"I'm here, Luis. Can you hear me?"

Had she imagined that faint twitch? Praying she hadn't, she murmured softly, "So much has happened the past few days. Flying statues. Visits to cardinals. Nightmares. Marriage proposals. With all that going on, I neglected to mention that I love you."

Breath suspended, she waited for a response. Any kind of a response. None came.

"I know," she whispered, forcing a smile into her voice. "It surprised me, too. All these weeks and months I've kept insisting we take things one step at a time. I didn't realize my subconscious was already eight steps ahead of me."

She raised his hand and took care to avoid the IV as she brushed her lips across it.

"You need to get well, my darling. We have a wedding to arrange."

The minutes between visits ticked by with agonizing slowness. Claire downed cup after cup of coffee and made a tentative attempt to communicate with the family huddled on the other side of the waiting room. The psychologist in her responded to their pain, even while her own threatened to choke her.

The youngest grandchild had studied English in school. She responded to Claire's overtures with a shy smile and soon had her siblings sharing stories about their *babička*. Their grandfather sat quietly all through the telling, his eyes sad and resigned.

Just before dawn, Claire got wearily to her feet to pour yet another cup of coffee. It was mostly sludge now, but it would give her system the jolt she needed for the next trip into the ICU. She was adding a third packet of sugar to the syrupy liquid when Lightning strode into the waiting room. With him was the slender woman Claire counted among her dearest friends.

"Maggie!"

Maggie Sinclair Ridgeway was the last person she expected to see in Prague. The one-time operative and former director of OMEGA served on a slew of charitable organizations in addition to keeping busy with her own career and always-busy family. What she insisted on labeling "character" lines now fanned out at the corners of her brown eyes, but her hair was the same luminous brown and her smile still lit up any room she walked into.

Coffee sloshed over Claire's hand as she tossed her cup into the wastebasket. When she rushed across the room, Maggie opened her arms and Claire fell into them. The woman who prided herself on maintaining strict control over her emotions—the psychologist who concealed every thought behind a calm mask—burst into noisy, racking sobs.

Maggie didn't try to check them. Cradling Claire in her arms, she rocked back and forth.

She and Cyrene had worked a number of ops together and Maggie considered this woman more than a friend. She was the sister she never had. She knew what Claire had gone through after her husband was murdered and could only imagine the paralyzing fear that had to be gripping her now.

Stroking her friend's silky blond hair, she murmured the empty promises everyone did during crises like this. "It's all right. He'll be all right."

"He has to be." Claire pulled back. Her tear-ravaged eyes were filled with despair. "I can't lose him, Maggie."

"I know."

She should. She'd been the lure that brought Luis to Washington, but Claire was the one he'd fallen for. Along with everyone else in OMEGA, Maggie had watched Esteban's determined pursuit over the years. She had to admit Claire had handled the sexy Latin American with a deft hand. Not an easy task, given the man's occasional lapses into Stone Age thinking when it came to little things like "his woman" going out on dangerous undercover ops.

"I love him," Claire sobbed. "More than I ever dreamed possible."

"I know," Maggie repeated, sending Lightning a glance over her friend's head. "Everyone does."

Claire drew back, blinking through her tears. "Wh… What?"

On cue, Lightning responded to Maggie's silent signal. "Don't tell me you didn't know about the pool?"

The diversionary tactic worked. Sniffling, Claire looked from him to Maggie and back again.

"Pool?"

"Everyone was betting on when you'll finally break down and agree to marry the poor guy. I think the pot's well over three hundred now. I've got next month," he added with a hopeful waggle of his brows. "The twentieth, to be exact. Think you can hold out until then?"

"Sorry." Still sniffling, Claire eased into a smile. "Who had yesterday?"

"Damn! Diamond, I think."

His hound-dog expression drew a watery chuckle from Claire and a huff from Maggie.

"Right." She grinned at the sophisticated millionaire who'd offered to act as her pimp when he was a half-starved twelve-year-old pickpocket. "Like you need the three hundred, Jensen."

Their banter gave Claire the time she needed to

recover her composure. "I was just going in to see Luis when you showed up. Come with me."

Maggie and Nick had both seen plenty of wounds and injuries during their years with OMEGA. She expected them to take the tubes and monitors in stride. Still, she tried to prepare them.

Nothing could prepare *her,* however, for the grim expression on the face of the doctor who exited the ICU just as they were about to enter.

He was young, in his middle thirties, and had come on duty an hour or so before Maggie and Lightning arrived. To Claire's relief, he'd pulled a surgical rotation at Atlanta's largest medical center and spoke English with the musical accent of a down-home, Southern Czech.

"Dr. Cantwell. I was just coming to look for you."

Claire's chest squeezed with pure, unadulterated terror. She groped for Maggie's hand. Lightning slid an arm around her shoulders.

"Why? What's happened?"

"Ambassador Esteban is awake and is now asking for you. I must say," he added as Claire rushed past, "he's what I would call a recalcitrant patient."

He didn't look recalcitrant, Claire thought, on a choking half sob. He looked pale and weak and stubborn as hell.

"There you are." He followed his hoarse croak with a grunt of surprise. "And you, Maggie!"

"And Nick," Claire said, rather unnecessarily,

as the three of them crowded around his bed. "Here, suck on some of this chipped ice. It'll ease your throat."

While she held the plastic cup to his lips, his dark eyes darted from Nick to Maggie. His throat worked as he swallowed the melted ice chip with an obviously painful effort.

"It is good you have come," he rasped. "I do not like—" grimacing, he swallowed again "—to leave Claire alone…until we know who hired… this Dawson."

"We know," Lightning replied.

Either Luis didn't hear or he was still too doped up for the startling reply to fully register. Or, Claire realized as he fumbled for her hand, he had a more pressing matter on his mind.

"Tell me," he demanded in that raw voice, "did you come to me? Did you say…what I have longed…to hear? Or was I…dreaming?"

Careful to avoid his IV line, she squeezed his hand gently. "You weren't dreaming."

Fierce satisfaction flared in his dark eyes. He looked so much like himself in that moment that the fear still clutching at the edges of Claire's mind evaporated.

Keeping a firm grip on her hand, he turned his attention to Nick. "Now, tell us what it is you know."

Chapter 12

Luis insisted he'd recovered enough to fly home a mere twenty-four hours later. Despite his doctor's reservations, he departed the hospital with his ribs taped and a bottle of prescription painkillers in his pocket.

Nick smoothed their departure by arranging a hurried meeting with the Czech investigators who needed to take Luis's statement. He also hired a licensed nurse to accompany them on the flight back to the States. Since this was done via the luxurious jet Nick chartered for his personal use, the flight home was both swift and uneventful.

Luis slept most of the way. The painkillers and

steady engine whine kept him out until they were on final approach to Washington's Reagan International.

"Luis." Claire nudged him gently. "Wake up. We're here."

Grimacing at the tug on his ribs, he brought his seat upright for landing. "What time is it?"

"Fifteen-ten local," Lightning replied with a glance at his sleek and very expensive watch.

Mere moments later, they taxied to a stop within sight of the stretch limo Nick had ordered. Once the customs officer who met the aircraft cleared them, Maggie had to separate from the rest of the group.

Not without regrets. Tucking a strand of warm brown hair behind her ear, she gave Luis a rueful grin. "Being in the field with you again brought back a few memories."

"Ah. You are thinking, perhaps, of the time you came to my country and disguised yourself in the garb of a streetwalker?"

"Actually, I'm thinking of the giant iguana you sent home with me after that particular mission. Terence made Adam's life miserable for years."

"It's no more than Ridgeway deserves for stealing you from me."

The reply was as smooth as the way he raised her hand to his lips. Neither the extravagant compliment nor the cosmopolitan gesture fooled either of the women present. They knew who held the keys to his heart.

"Call me," Maggie instructed Claire. "We'll down sour-apple martinis and talk wedding plans."

Once in the limo, Claire didn't bother to suggest they drop Luis off at either her place or the embassy residence to rest. First, he would flat-out refuse. Second, he had as much a stake in the events of the next hour or so as she did.

Her nerves tightened in grim anticipation as the limo left the airport and glided along the GW Parkway. The route took them by the Pentagon and across the 14th Street Bridge. The Jefferson Memorial gleamed in the bright May sunshine, its round dome and graceful columns silhouetted against the blue-green waters of the Tidal Basin. Once across the bridge, the limo driver eased through afternoon traffic.

Claire's nerves tightened another notch when they passed the soaring obelisk of the Washington Monument and the White House came into view. Nick had radioed from out over the Atlantic to set up a meeting with President Andrews, his vice president and his chief of staff. The meeting, she knew, would have unprecedented ramifications.

When the limo pulled up at the first White House checkpoint, Claire had a startling sense of déjà vu. She and Nick had stopped at this same checkpoint a scant few weeks ago. It seemed more like years, given everything that had happened since. Her consults with Stacy Andrews. All the tests she and her colleagues had run on the teen. The attack outside Claire's condo. The trip to Prague with its near-disastrous results.

Well, not all disastrous. She glanced at Luis's handsome, determined face and felt the knot in her stomach ease a bit. Whatever came of this meeting, whatever drastic changes occurred because of it, one constant would remain. Her hand slid across the cloud-soft leather and slipped into his.

He slanted her a quick look and even quicker smile. "Soon it will be over," he murmured as the driver pulled up at the second checkpoint. "Then we will make time for us."

She kept that promise in mind while a security officer issued badges and escorted them to the West Wing. Claire had met with the president in the Oval Office once before. Still, she couldn't fail to feel the history imbued in its walls and furnishings as the receptionist showed her, Luis and Nick in.

As requested, the vice president and chief of staff were already present, as was the president. Daniel Molineaux and Tom Fogarty rose while John Andrews came around from behind his desk to shake Luis's good hand.

"We heard you took a bullet in Prague, Ambassador Esteban."

"A bullet," Luis drawled, "and almost a saint."

"Come again?"

"It's of no importance now. We have more pressing matters to discuss."

"So Nick said. Please, have a seat."

He gestured to the chairs and sofas grouped around a low table. Claire took the seat beside Luis, Nick the chair opposite the president. That left the VP and the chief of staff side by side on the sofa.

The silver-maned Dan Molineaux had served in Washington too long to show either undue curiosity or impatience. Tom Fogarty, on the other hand, unleashed both.

"We had to cut the president's press conference short and put a follow-on meeting with the Congressional Budget Office on hold to fit you in, Dr. Cantwell. I hope whatever you uncovered in Prague is worth it."

"We think it is," she replied coolly.

The president was more concerned about his daughter than the press conference or the adjustments to his schedule.

"Start at the beginning," he instructed Claire tersely. "Don't leave anything out. I want to know exactly what happened over there."

She'd expected Lightning to take the lead but a

nod from him confirmed this was her show. Collecting her thoughts, she complied with the president's demand.

"As you know, sir, we met with the archbishop of Prague the day after we arrived in the Czech Republic. Unfortunately, Cardinal Tuma couldn't pinpoint with any accuracy the root cause of Stacy's nightmares."

The president's jaw worked. "That's what Nick told us."

"However, the cardinal's assistant did confirm Stacy's great-grandfather was from a town about an hour outside Prague. It's called Sedlec."

The name didn't register with the president. He shook his head and Claire continued.

"Father Milosec gave us directions before we left the palace. On our way out was when we had a close encounter with a falling saint," she added dryly. "St. Benedict, to be precise."

Andrews looked taken aback, his chief of staff confused. The vice president, Claire noted, showed no reaction at all. After so many decades in Washington, the man had learned well how to mask his thoughts.

"I mention Benedict only because the individual who deliberately dislodged the statue from the roof of the archbishop's palace also made a visit to Sedlec some months ago. He and his partner, Ed Porter."

"Porter?"

"The man who attacked Luis and me outside my condo."

That sparked reactions from all three men. The president swore, the VP's eyes narrowed, and the chief of staff stiffened.

"Are you implying this is some kind of conspiracy?" Fogarty said incredulously.

"I'm not implying anything," Claire shot back. "I'm stating a fact."

"Jesus!" Fogarty shook his head. "What proof do you have?"

"Dawson signed the register at the church. That's not his real name, of course."

"I don't get it." The president shagged a hand through his hair. "What were these guys, Dawson and Porter, doing in the Czech Republic?"

"We suspect they were digging into the same thing Colonel Esteban and I were, sir. The source of your wife's—and subsequently your daughter's—nightmares."

"The hell you say! How would two thugs like these know Teo had nightmares as a child?"

Claire's eyes hardened. So did her voice. She was Cyrene now, ice calm and tasting blood. "We asked ourselves the same question and put an entire team at OMEGA on it. They found a reference to Mrs. Andrews's childhood sleep disturbance in the medical history she completed your first year in office as governor."

The president's brows snapped together. "Aside from the fact that medical histories are supposed to be protected by privacy laws, I still don't understand Porter and Dawson's role in all this."

The tension swirling through the room was like a living thing, sinuous and all-pervasive. Claire felt it in every nerve as she leaned forward.

"You need more of their background to make the connection, sir. Dawson served in the British army during the first Gulf War, went mercenary in the second. That's where he hooked up with Porter. The two joined forces and hired themselves out as personal bodyguards for a series of Iraqi officials."

She kept her attention focused on the president, yet her every sense was attuned to the two men on sofa opposite her.

"While in Iraq, Dawson and Porter came to the attention of certain officials in the Department of Defense. They flew the men back to the States at least twice for secret meetings, at which time they were issued a charter that allowed them to operate outside the rules of engagement constraining both our military and the CIA."

"Outside, how?" the president asked sharply.

"Dawson and Porter evolved into a two-person hit squad. We believe they're responsible for three assassinations in Iraq and two in Syria. They've since widened their area of operations. Interpol thinks they may have struck in Paris and Amsterdam, as well."

Andrews swore and whipped his attention to his second in command. "You served as secretary of defense during some of that, Dan. Did any hint of a private death squad ever reach your ears?"

The snowy-haired politician's gaze shifted from the president to Claire. Their eyes met, held. She broke the silent standoff with a low warning.

"Tell him, Mr. Vice President, or we will."

He regarded her for another few seconds without so much as a flicker of emotion. Then he acknowledged the link with a dip of his head.

"I met with them, John. Both times. As OMEGA has obviously uncovered. But there was no charter issued by me or anyone in my office. What they did, they did on their own."

A low hiss escaped from Luis and Nick's jaw went tight, but they let Claire deliver the coup de grâce.

"I expect Porter and Dawson knew you would disclaim any knowledge of their activities if or when they were caught, Mr. Vice President. That must be why Dawson recorded his conversation with the head of a lobby representing the NRA on March second of this year."

Claire dropped the bombshell without taking her eyes off Daniel Molineaux.

"In that conversation," she continued, "the lobbyist claimed the strict gun controls President Andrews wants to implement would strip individual citizens of the right to bear arms."

"So?" The VP shrugged. "The president is well aware of my more conservative views on the issue of gun control. We've agreed to disagree on this matter."

He was good. Damned good. He had to be sweating under his pinstriped suit and silk tie, but no one could have guessed it to look at him. That's what years in Washington did for a politician, Claire thought as she plunged the knife in.

"In the same conversation, this lobbyist claimed you personally suggested Dawson and Porter as the right men to engineer President Andrews's resignation."

"What?"

The president went rigid with shock and dawning fury. From the corner of her eye, she saw his shoulders square and his fists bunch. Her own hands clenched tight as she unraveled the last strands in the sick plot.

"OMEGA found the recorded conversations in a safety-deposit box leased in one of Dawson's aliases. Also in the box was a memo noting the make and serial number of the iPod Dawson purchased at the lobbyist's direction. The one the lobbyist said you intended to substitute for Stacy's."

She leaned forward, her eyes stabbing into his.

"What's on that iPod, Mr. Vice President? Subliminal messages? Frightening images embedded in Stacy's favorite music videos? You might as well tell us. We'll find out anyway when her Secret Service detail delivers the iPod, as we've requested."

The silver-maned politician's gaze made a slow circle of those around him. From Tom Fogarty, who wore a stunned expression and was leaning sideways over the arm of the sofa, as if to distance himself from the man, to Lightning to Luis to Claire. Finally, he met the narrow-eyed stare of the man he'd battled so fiercely in the primaries.

"The iPod contains a miniature receiver tuned to a single, shielded frequency," he admitted in a stony voice lacking its usual resonance. "Porter tested it the first time in Cartoza. He booked a room in the hotel across the square from the presidential palace and used the shielded channel to send subtle, frightening messages when Stacy was asleep."

"You son of a bitch!"

John Andrews lunged out of his chair. Fogarty yelped and flung himself sideways as the president hauled back a fist and slammed it into his vice president's jaw.

* * *

Two hours later, it was all over but the shouting.

That would come, Fogarty predicted, as soon as the media got wind of the bizarre scheme. He departed the president's office with the White House counsel and a still somewhat stunned press secretary, to put together a draft statement.

That left Lightning, Luis and Claire to accompany the president when he went to inform his daughter of the plot. The teen watched with mounting confusion when the chief of White House security confiscated her iPod and dropped it into an evidence bag.

"What's going on, Dad?"

"Sit down, Stacy, and I'll tell you."

With a bewildered look at the other three, she perched on the edge of the sofa. Her jaw sagged as her father described the bizarre plot. When he'd finished, a flush of healthy anger stained her cheeks.

"Where did Mr. Molineaux and his dorky friends get off, trying to use me to make you resign? I hope they all go to jail. For a long, long time!"

"They will," Andrews promised, tugging on a hank of her hair with a hand showing bruised knuckles.

She savored the pleasure in that promise for several moments, before voicing a new concern. "You're going to get me another iPod, right? I want an iPod Touch this time."

"We'll talk about that later. Right now, don't you think you should thank Dr. Cantwell and Colonel Esteban for everything they went through on your behalf?"

Seeing the worry wiped from the teen's eyes was thanks enough for Claire. Luis, however, had a special request.

"It's because of you that I have finally convinced Claire to be my wife. You will come to our wedding, yes?"

"Yes!"

Chapter 13

With Maggie Sinclair's help, Claire managed to pull off the relatively small wedding she'd envisioned. No mean feat, given that the president, his daughter, their Secret Service details and every OMEGA agent not currently in the field attended.

The location helped foster the illusion of intimacy. Maggie and Adam had offered the use of their MacLean, Virginia, home. With its lush landscaping and latticework gazebo, the backyard provided a setting fragrant with the scent of roses and gardenias. Its wide flagstone terraces also allowed for banks of white folding chairs to seat guests.

Luckily, the weather cooperated. Bright June

sunlight filtered through the leafy maples shading the yard as the guests mingled on the terraces prior to the ceremony. In addition to the OMEGA crew, the D.C. diplomatic corps was well represented, as were Luis's friends and relatives. His brother had flown up from Cartoza with his lively young family. Luis's great-aunt, Tia Maria, accompanied them. The feisty ninety-two-year-old came into the room where Claire was dressing to offer some blunt advice on handling her husband-to-be.

"He is not like other men, that one. He will demand much of you, in bed and out."

Her mouth curved. "So I've discovered."

Tia Maria's shrewd eyes raked the bride's face. "I know you have loved once and lost. Luis will help heal the pain of that loss."

Claire bent to brush her lips across the woman's wrinkled cheek. "He already has," she said softly.

That thought stayed with her during the final moments it took for Maggie to pin a spray of lilies of the valley in Claire's upswept hair, and adjust the short, lace bolero jacket that topped her sleeveless, ivory satin sheath. It was still there when the music swelled and Lightning offered his arm to escort her out onto the terrace.

Luis was waiting on the steps of the gazebo with his brother beside him. As always, Claire's stomach fluttered at the mere sight of his impossibly handsome face. Then his silky black mustache tipped up in a smile that filled every corner of her mind, and he stepped forward to tuck her arm in his.

"Te adoro, mi esposa."

The murmur was for her ears alone. Claire took care not to press too closely against his still-bandaged ribs as she answered straight from her heart.

"Te adoro, my husband."

* * * * *

Bestselling author Lynne Graham is back
with a fabulous new trilogy!

PREGNANT BRIDES

Three ordinary girls—naive, but also honest and plucky…

Three fabulously wealthy, impossibly handsome
and very ruthless men…

When opposites attract and passion leads to pregnancy…
it can only mean marriage!

Available next month from Harlequin Presents®:
the first installment

DESERT PRINCE, BRIDE OF INNOCENCE

* * *

'THIS EVENING I'm flying to New York for two weeks,'
Jasim imparted with a casualness that made her heart sink
like a stone. 'That's why I had you brought here. I own this
apartment and you'll be comfortable here while I'm abroad.'

'I can afford my own accommodation although I may not
need it for long. I'll have another job by the time you
get back—'

Jasim released a slightly harsh laugh. 'There's no need for
you to look for another position. How would I ever see you?
Don't you understand what I'm offering you?'

Elinor stood very still. 'No, I must be incredibly thick
because I haven't quite worked out yet what you're offering
me.…'

His charismatic smile slashed his lean dark visage.
'Naturally, I want to take care of you.…'

'No, thanks.' Elinor forced a smile and mentally willed him not to demean her with some sordid proposition. 'The only man who will ever take *care* of me with my agreement will be my husband. I'm willing to wait for you to come back but I'm not willing to be kept by you. I'm a very independent woman and what I give, I give freely.'

Jasim frowned. 'You make it all sound so serious.'

'What happened between us last night left pure chaos in its wake. Right now, I don't know whether I'm on my head or my heels. I'll stay for a while because I have nowhere else to go in the short term. So maybe it's good that you'll be away for a while.'

Jasim pulled out his wallet to extract a card. 'My private number,' he told her, presenting her with it as though it was a precious gift, which indeed it was. Many women would have done just about anything to gain access to that direct hotline to him, but his staff guarded his privacy with scrupulous care.

Before he could close the wallet, his blood ran cold in his veins. How could he have made such a serious oversight? What if he had got her pregnant? He knew that an unplanned pregnancy would engulf his life like an avalanche, crush his freedom and suffocate him. He barely stilled a shudder at the threat of such an outcome and thought how ironic it was that what his older brother had longed and prayed for to secure the line to the throne should strike Jasim as an absolute disaster....

* * *

What will proud Prince Jasim do if Elinor is expecting his royal baby? Perhaps an arranged marriage is the only solution! But will Elinor agree? Find out in DESERT PRINCE, BRIDE OF INNOCENCE by Lynne Graham [#2884], available from Harlequin Presents® in January 2010.

HPEX0110B

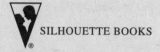

SILHOUETTE BOOKS

PLEASE RECYCLE
THIS PRODUCT IS RECYCLABLE

Recycling programs for this product may not exist in your area.

ISBN-13: 978-0-373-27659-2

SEDUCED BY THE OPERATIVE

Visit Silhouette Books at www.eHarlequin.com

Printed in U.S.A.

MERLINE LOVELACE

Seduced by the Operative

Silhouette®
Romantic
SUSPENSE

Dear Reader,

As many of you know, Claire Cantwell, code name Cyrene, and sexy Colonel Luis Esteban have appeared as secondary characters in a number of CODE NAME: DANGER novels. I plotted their book years ago, but other projects kept getting in the way. So many readers have asked for their story, though, that I've—finally!—written it. I hope you have as much fun as I did going along on the mission that tested both Claire's skills and her ability to resist Luis's determined pursuit.

If you'd like to see photos of the places and events described in this book, go to my Web site at www.merlinelovelace.com and click on the Travel tab at the top of the page, then on the album labeled Europe '07.

And be sure to watch for the next CODE NAME: DANGER book, coming in 2010 from the Silhouette Romantic Suspense line.

All my best,

Merline

"What if I stay longer?"

He gave her hair another slow stroke. "Or don't leave at all?" The question brought her blinking awake, as he'd known it would. Pushing upright, she propped herself on an elbow. Her hair fell across her forehead. When she hooked the loose strand behind her ear, he saw her face clearly in the moonlight streaming through the top half of plantation shutters. Saw, too, the question in her eyes.

"We agreed up front that we both need our space, Luis. We discussed boundaries."

"Perhaps it's time to renegotiate those boundaries."

"Why?"

"I want more of you, Claire."

"You have all I'm prepared to give right now," she said quietly. "All I *can* give."

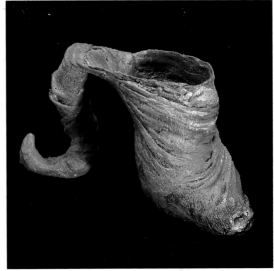

Angelo Rinaldi,
Cenerentolo
(Cinderfella),
Murano glass,
Florence 1993.

Danielle Stephane,
Vestale
(Vestal virgin),
fabric,
Lione 1992.

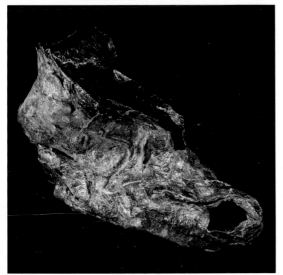

Martin Canneel,
*On the way to
Bodgaya,*
paper,
Brussels 1993.

FOLLOWING PAGE
Angelo Barcella,
Scarpante
(Kicky shoe),
mixed materials,
Milan 1993.

PRECEDING PAGE
Aldo Mondino,
Cicli e ricicli
(Cycle and recycle),
mixed materials,
Turin 1993.

Giuseppe Scala,
Groviglio
(Tangle),
wire,
Syracuse 1993.

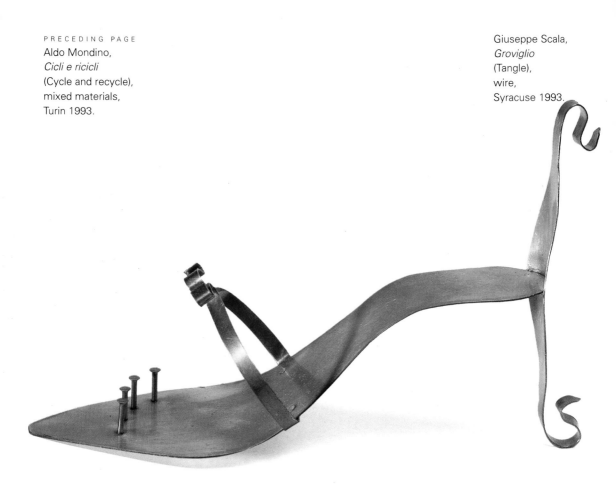

Gianni Mantovani,
Silhouette,
brass,
Modena 1993.

Ferruccio D'Angelo,
Sottovuoto
(Vacuum packed),
aluminum and velvet,
Turin 1992.

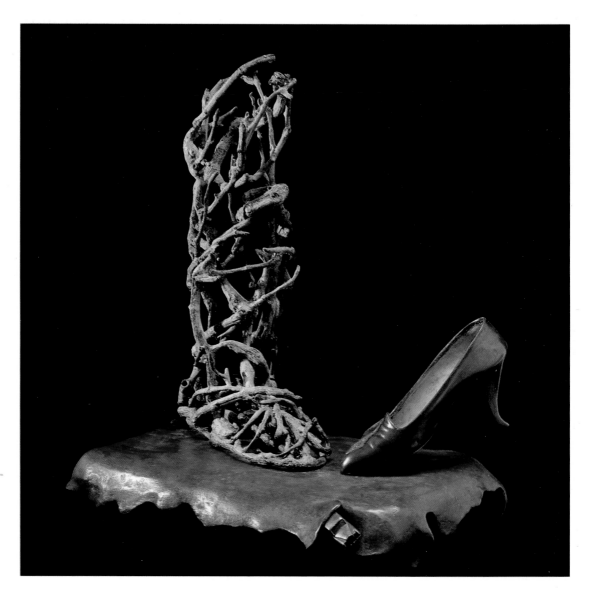

Giancarlo Montuschi,
Notte e giorno
(Night and day),
ceramic,
Perugia 1993.

Cosimo Cimino,
Men's inside,
mixed materials,
La Spezia 1993.

Fabio De Sanctis,
Paradiso pedestre
(Heaven on foot),
bronze,
Rome 1993.

Denis D'Elia,
Cammino
(On the road),
metal and terracotta,
Rimini 1992.

89

Emilio Isgrò,
Untitled,
mixed materials,
Milan 1993.

Novello Finotti,
Piano piano... lontano
(Slow and steady
wins the race),
terracotta and wood,
Verona 1993.

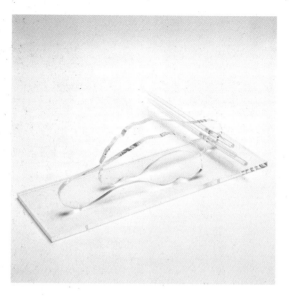

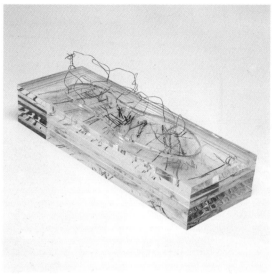

Nakis Tastsioglou,
Achille
(Achilles),
Plexiglas,
Athens 1993.

Donatella Mei,
Fuga dagli Uffizi
(Escape from the
Uffizi),
Plexiglas,
Florence 1993.

Candida Ferrari,
Le soulier de satin
(Satin shoe),
Plexiglas,
Parma 1993.

Elio Di Franco,
Shoes Eiffel
(Eiffel shoes),
brass and Plexiglas,
Florence 1993.

Ogata,
Impronta
(Essence),
marble,
La Spezia 1993.

Ezio Gribaudo,
Untitled,
wood and leather,
Turin 1993.

Gianni Ambrogio,
*All'affannosa ricerca
di Cenerentola*
(Desperately seeking
Cinderella),
mixed materials,
Treviso 1993.

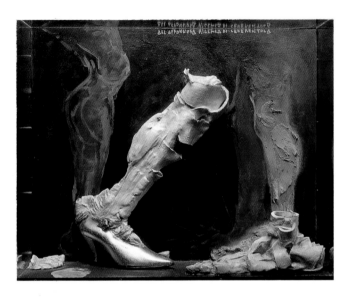

Mario Mariotti,
Antipodi
(Antipodes),
cement, rubber, and
wood,
Florence 1993.

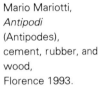

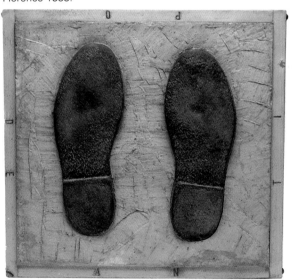

Mirella Bentivoglio and Gisella Meo,
*Una scarpa di pagine/Favola come
utopia/Lapide a Cenerentola*
(A literary shoe/Fairy tale turns out to
be fairy tale/Cinderella's tombstone),
marble and glass,
Rome 1993.

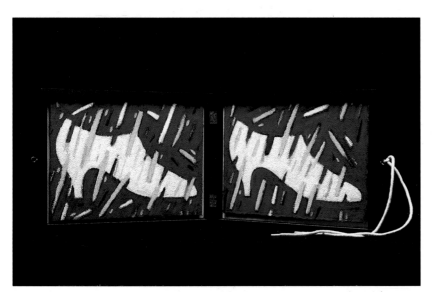

Giulio Telarico,
Untitled,
oil on wood,
Cosenza 1993.

Paolo Cotza,
Passo acustico
(Audible steps),
brass and wood,
Turin 1993.

Brunivo Buttarelli,
Untitled,
wood and metal,
Cremona 1993.

Giuseppe Calonaci,
Macchina del sole
(Sun machine),
mixed materials,
Siena 1992.

PRECEDING PAGE
Tina Karageorgi,
Untitled,
wood,
Athens 1993.

99

Francesco Colacicchi,
Naufragio
(Shipwrecked),
mixed materials,
Florence 1993.

Silvina Spravkin,
Seta pesante
(Heavy silk),
marble,
Carrara 1993.

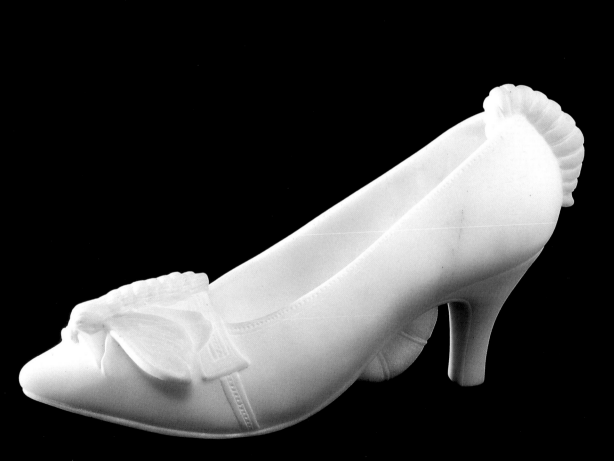

Philip Tsiaras,
Grecian shoe vase,
ceramic and leather,
New York 1991.

Irene Kalogheris,
Mediterraneo
(Mediterranean),
plastic, leather,
and marble,
Patras 1993.

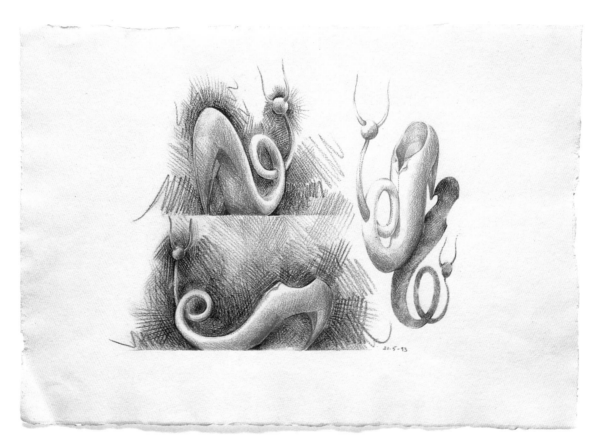

William Sawaya,
Scarpa curiosa
(Odd shoe),
Milan 1993.

104

Design

Not functional, although appropriate to the theme of the project. Shoe-shaped, then, even if surreal and Neo-Baroque, playful and Neo-Pop, technological and Post-Modern, radical and Neo-Modern. A dictionary of all the languages of design; an innocuous Tower of Babel, where cultured languages and dialects are echoed; an intentionally uncoordinated repertory of creators, protagonists, and second leads, taking care to shift their own message onto the shoe, the symbol par excellence: some have gone along with the game and played around, while others have taken it seriously, transforming the exercise of invention into a declaration of intent.

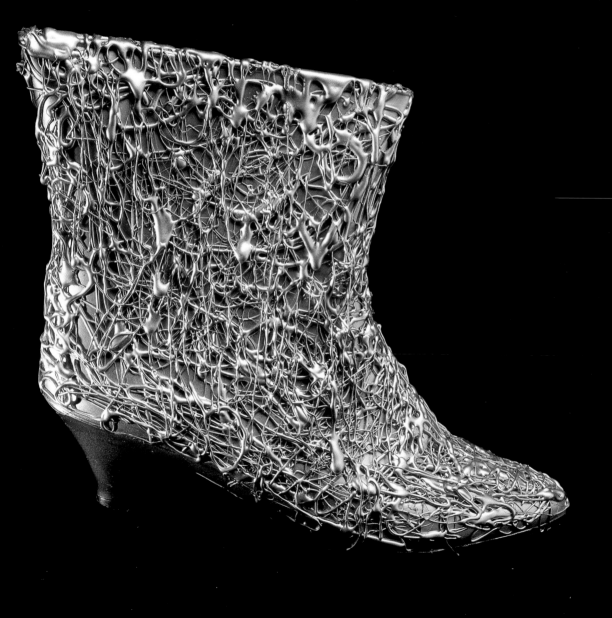

Stefano Giovannoni,
Impermeabile
(Impermeable),
plastic and silicone,
Milan 1993

Lapo Binazzi,
Strade d'Italia
(Roads of Italy),
rubber,
Florence 1993.

Antonio Dattis,
Lorenzo il Magnifico
(Lorenzo the
Magnificent),
wire netting and
feather,
Florence 1992.

Nicola Falcone,
Victoria,
metal,
Florence 1992.

Marco Lucidi
Pressanti,
Flower power,
fabric,
Florence 1992

Tarshito,
Radicata
(Deep-rooted),
ceramic and brass,
Bari 1993.

Andrée Putman for
Charles Jourdan,
Untitled,
suede,
Paris 1992.

Val Jones
The real macaw,
leather and feathers,
London 1992.

L'Aquilone
Hillary,
ceramic,
Florence 1992.

Lars Hagen,
Vanity,
mirrors,
Kassel 1991.

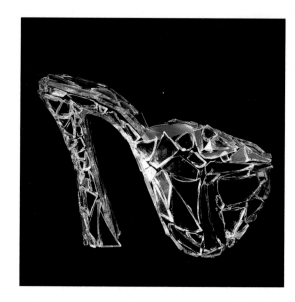

Cristina Burzio,
The lady in red,
ceramic,
Florence 1993.

Archimede Seguso
for Bruno Magli,
Trasparenza
(Transparency),
Murano glass,
Murano 1980.

Andrés Salas Acosta
and Glorimar
Santiago,
Silver shadow,
metal,
Puerto Rico 1991.

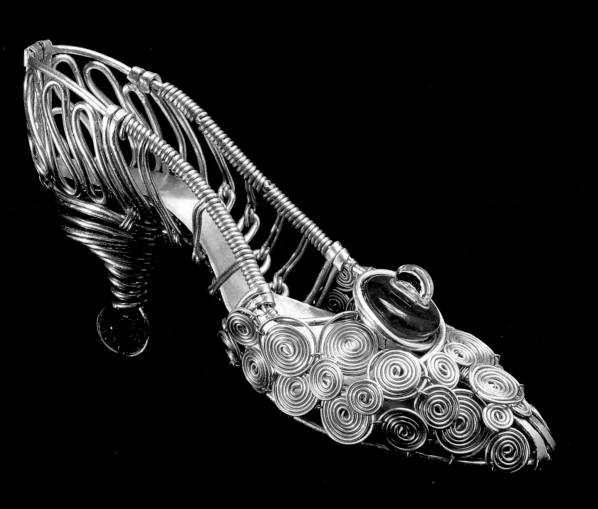

Giorgio Vigna,
Italia
(Italy),
leather and paper,
Milan 1993.

Maurizio Cosua,
Mal d'Africa
(Sick for Africa),
paper, wood, and
leather,
Venice 1993.

Girolamo Palmizi,
Italia
(Italy),
papier-maché
Milan 1991.

Karim Azzabi,
Sole,
plastic,
Milan 1993.

Edgar Vallora,
Crocodile shoe,
painted wood,
Milan 1993.

Ludwig Hartmann,
Scarctcus
(Prickly pump),
clay, wood, and
plastic,
Ecuador 1991.

Pino Milella,
Anfibio
(Amphibious),
rope and plastic,
Bari 1992.

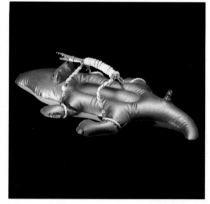

116

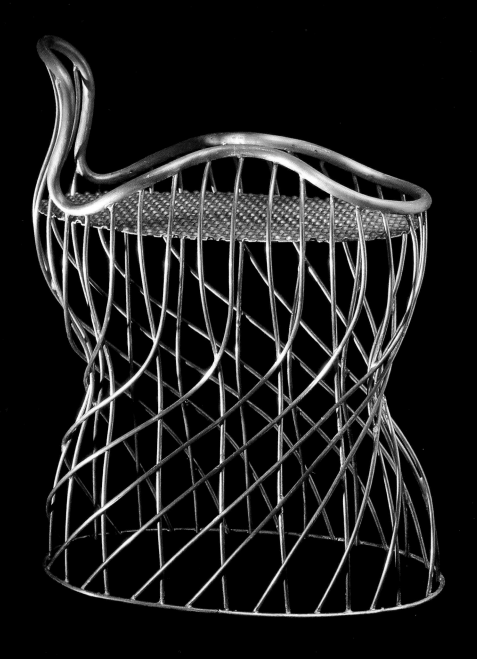

Massimo Monini,
Enigma,
silver,
Arezzo 1991.

Giuseppe Alleruzzo,
Gloria
(Glory),
metal,
Pistoia 1992.

Dafne Koz,
Cage,
brass,
Ankara 1993.

Maurizio Favetta with Thomas Kee and Micaela Eger,
Earth, wind, water, and fire,
mixed materials,
Milan 1992.

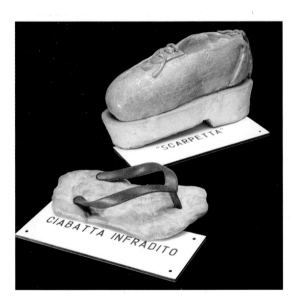

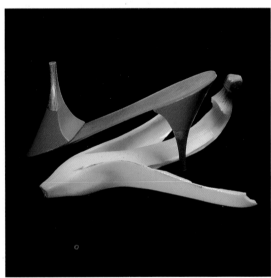

Angelo Jelmini,
Scarpetta e ciabatta
(Gravy wader and
flatbread flip-flop),
bread and rubber,
Milan 1992.

Riccardo Misesti,
Sabotage,
glass and plastic,
Arezzo 1992.

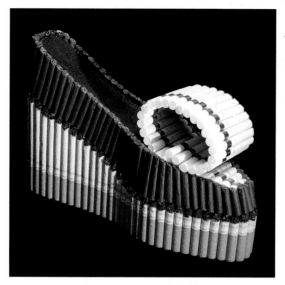

Russell Hall,
One foot in the grave,
cigarettes,
London 1992.

Wunderkammer,
Tiffany,
paper and iron,
Milan 1991.

Sandra Laube,
Sirena
(Mermaid),
plastic and spangles,
Florence 1992.

Kicca D'Ercole,
A kiss is just a kiss,
clay and tin foil,
Milan 1991.

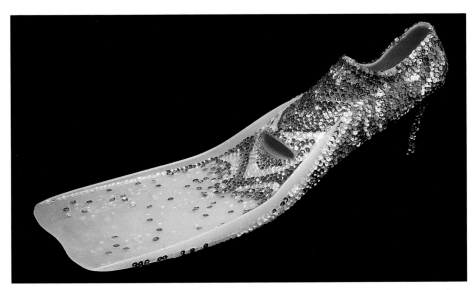

Shaun Clarkson,
She sells sea shells on the sea shore,
shells and leather,
London 1992.

Marco Belli,
Diecimila passi sotto i mari
(Twenty thousand steps under the sea),
metal and silicone,
Prato 1993.

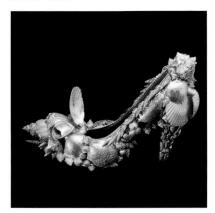

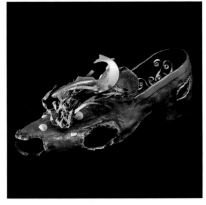

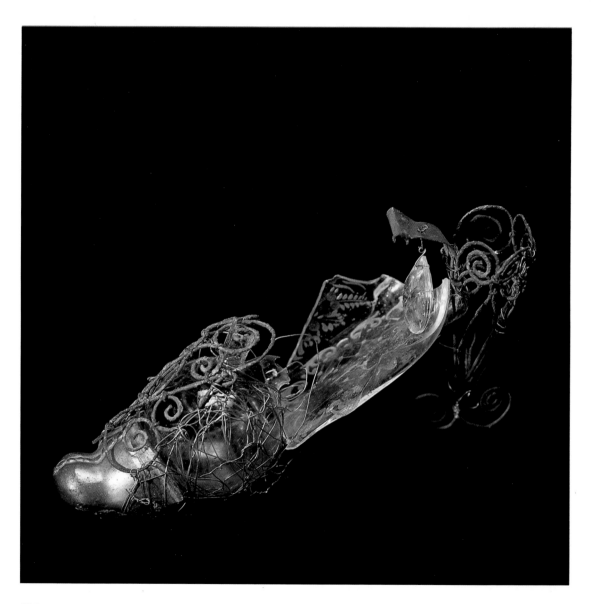

Ritsue Mishima,
Rococò,
glass and wood,
Venice 1991.

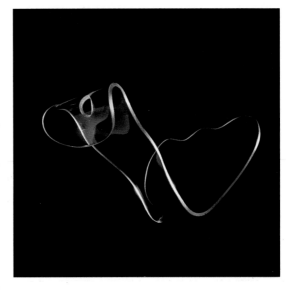

Nanda Vigo,
Scinderella 2500
(Cinderella 2500),
bent glass,
Milan 1993.

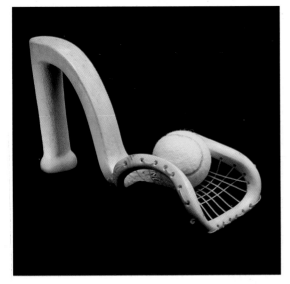

Claudia Bellini,
Martina,
wood, net, and tennis
ball,
Florence 1992.

Giulio and Valerio Vinaccia,
Stivaletti Super-Mario
(Super Mario boots),
leather and electronic
components
Milan 1992.

Mario Bottinelli Montandon,
I'm still waiting for a miracle,
leather and hi-fi components,
Como 1993.

Roberto Muscinelli,
Shoe shine,
leather and bulbs,
Milan 1992.

Pino Deodato,
Entità azzurra
(Blue being),
papier-maché and
pigment,
Milan 1993.

Maria Mollica,
Stregata
(Bewitched),
resin,
Milan 1993.

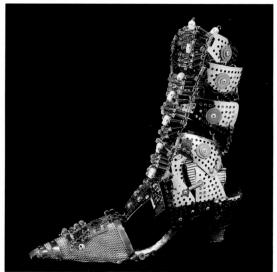

Monica Leoncini,
Cleopatra,
metal, leather, and
wood,
Florence 1991.

Regine De La Hey,
Ready made,
metals,
London 1992.

Gianfranco Pagnelli,
Balsamica
(Balsamic),
wood and leather,
Bari 1993.

Sabine Lercher,
Allegra ma non troppo
(Lively, but not too fast),
wood,
Bolzano 1993.

Fernando Andolcetti,
Schu-Bert shoe,
mixed materials,
La Spezia 1993.

Licia Dotti,
Piano, piano
(Slow stride piano),
wood,
Rome 1992.

Simonetta Starrabba,
La Bella e la Bestia
(Beauty and the Beast),
wood and buttons,
Rome 1993.

132

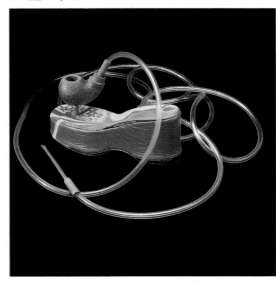

Maurizio De Caro,
Cubismo
(Cubism),
metal,
Milan 1993.

Viviana Di Blasi,
Smoking feet,
leather, wood, and
plastic,
Varese 1992.

Lucretia Moroni,
Where is your gravity center?,
paper and resin,
Milan 1993.

FOLLOWING PAGE
Massimo Iosa Ghini,
Aereodinamica
(Aerodynamic),
drawing and prototype of a chalk sole,
Milan 1990.

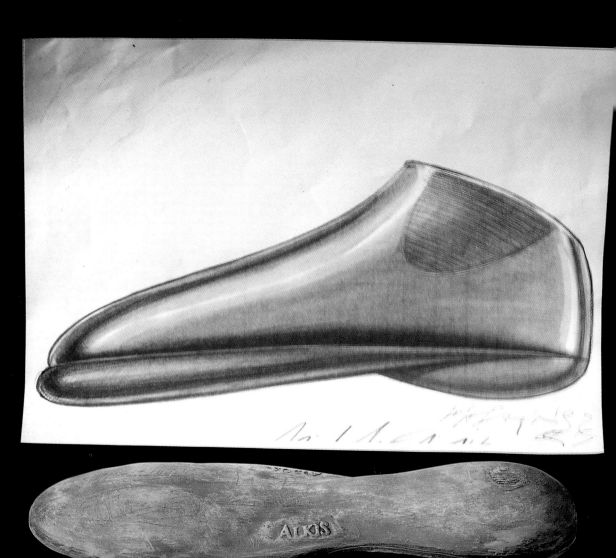

Alchimia A. Mendini
and A. Guerriero,
Decoro
(Decorum),
painted leather,
Milan 1988.

Giacomo Sanfilippo,
Nordsudestovest
(Northsoutheastwest),
wood and fabric,
Florence 1991.

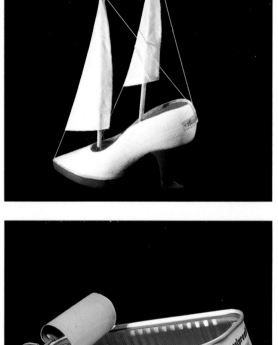

Mirella Jacovangelo,
Non calpestate i fiori
(Keep off the grass),
mixed materials,
Bergamo 1993.

Maria Gallo,
Alice,
tin,
Milan 1992.

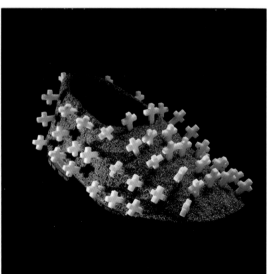

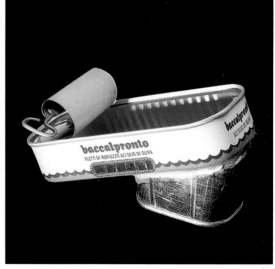

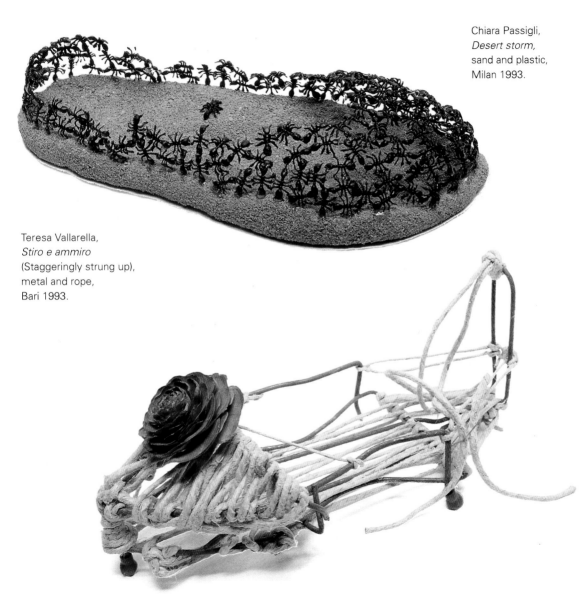

Chiara Passigli,
Desert storm,
sand and plastic,
Milan 1993.

Teresa Vallarella,
Stiro e ammiro
(Staggeringly strung up),
metal and rope,
Bari 1993.

Silvia Beghè,
Vulcanica
(Volcanic),
ceramic,
San Gimignano 1993.

Andrea Branzi,
Hard steps,
mixed materials,
Milan 1993.

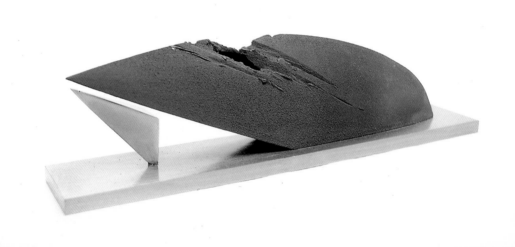

Marisa Korzeniecki,
Paesaggio con lago
(Landscape with lake),
iron and stainless
steel,
Ascoli Piceno 1993.

Biagio Cisotti for
Docksteps,
Fred Astaire,
leather and remote
control,
Florence 1993.

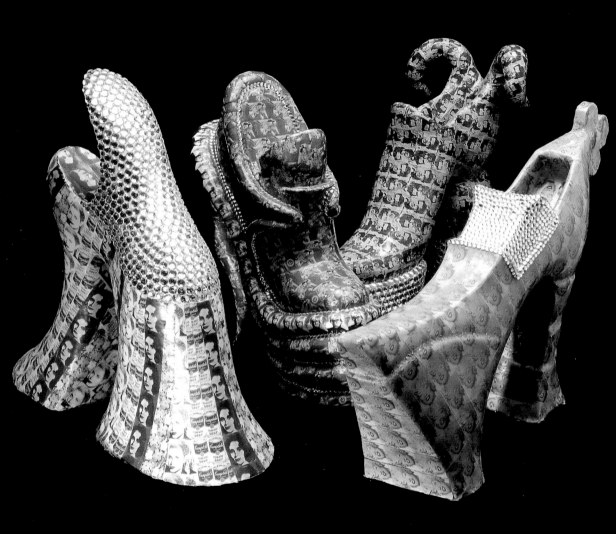

Simon Chalmers,
Jane's shoe,
plush, cardboard, and
leather,
London 1993.

PRECEDING PAGE
Giuseppe Arcofora,
In vino veritas,
glass and lead,
Syracuse 1992.

Isabella Santacroce,
Andy's shoes,
ceramic and
spangles,
Riccione 1993.

Christian Mounger,
Piede a spillo,
(Foot with spike heel),
wood and iron,
Los Angeles 1992.

Fausto Ghemi,
Percorso obbligato
(Mandatory course),
mixed materials,
Turin 1993.

Silvia Cappelletti and
Dora Grieco,
Leather is murder,
plastic,
Florence 1993.

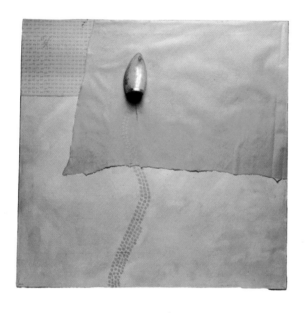

147

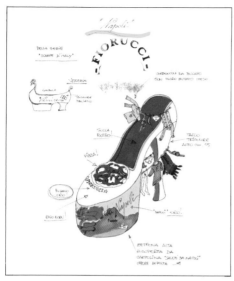

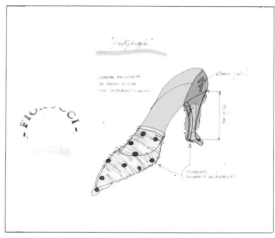

Elio Fiorucci,
Drawings,
Milan 1993.

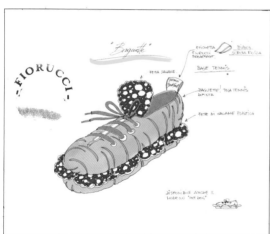

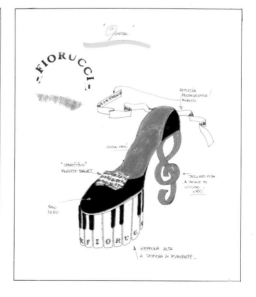

Fashion

Eventually, to wear. To exhibit, to show off in the game of seduction and allusion. Hoisted up to dizzy heights to excite the gaze. To walk, but above all to seduce. It seems that for stylists the shoe is an invitation to transgress; in this symbol there is, barely concealed, the concentrated desire to cross the threshold of good taste and moderation, and the hidden, slightly sadistic craving to force women to perform impossible balancing acts, to do harsh carnal penance. There may even be the hidden intention to provide shoes for fairies and imps: perhaps the secret desire of every stylist is to meet a new Cinderella.

Manolo Blahnik,
Man Ray style shoe,
mixed materials,
London 1991.

Bruno Magli,
Metropolis,
leather and metal,
Bologna 1980.

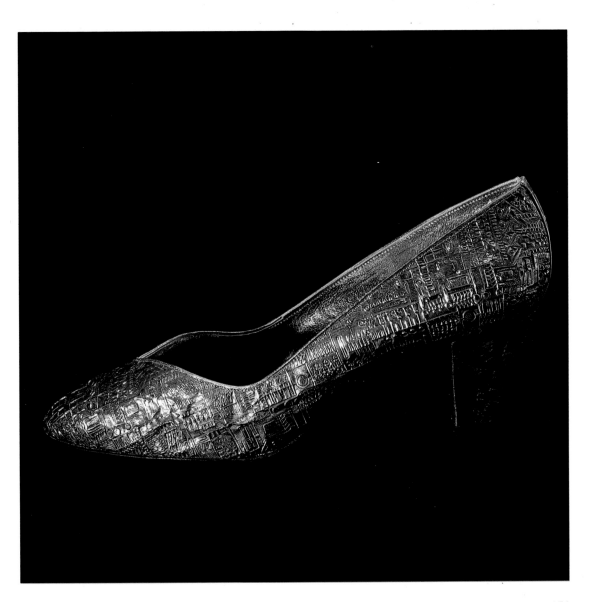

Romeo Gigli,
Folk,
fabric and mirrors,
Milan 1991.

Prevata by Azimut,
See through,
net,
Florence 1993.

Jean Paul Gaultier,
Palafitta
(Pump on pilings),
jet and plastic,
Paris 1993.

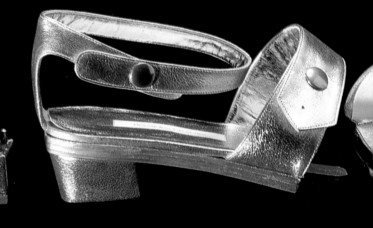

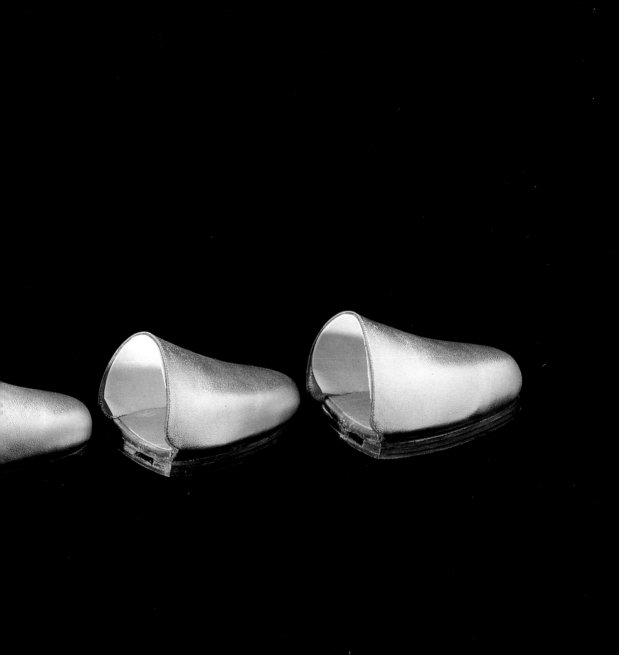

Jean Yves Malbos for
Osvaldo Martini,
Universale
(Universal),
leather,
Florence 1993.

Maria Gloria Bianchi
for Alberto Guardiani,
Anima gentile
(Gentle sole),
leather and ceramic,
Florence 1993.

Maurizio Dori,
Ambivalenza
(Ambivalence),
leather, fabric,
and metals,
Florence 1993.

Sergio Faccin,
La signora di Shangai
(The lady from
Shanghai),
glass,
Rome 1991.

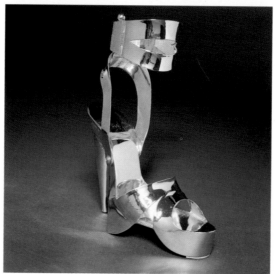

Thierry Mugler,
Bionic woman,
metal,
Paris 1992.

Vivienne Westwood,
Step by step,
leather and wood,
London 1993.

Luigino Rossi,
*Scarparotta
fraudolenta*
(Skipped town with
the funds),
wood and plastic,
Padua 1992.

Bernard Sucheras for
Charles Jourdan,
Soulier miniature
(Miniature shoe),
metal and fabric,
Paris 1991.

Azzedine Alaia,
Black lady,
suede and velvet,
Paris 1992.

Maria Gloria Bianchi
for Manas,
Déjeuner sur l'herbe
(Lunch on the grass),
mixed materials,
Florence 1993.

Gianni Bravo,
Temptation,
leather and plastic,
Ascoli Piceno 1993.

Stefano Bemer,
Le tre sgrazie,
(The Three Clumsies),
patent leather,
Florence 1993.

Claudia Ciuti,
Fossilizata
(Fossilized),
leather,
Pisa 1993.

Aroldo Marinai,
Anda e rianda
(Coming and going),
leather,
Florence 1992.

Henry Beguelin,
Prima posizione
(First position),
leather,
Milan 1993.

Travel Fox,
Rap shoe,
mixed materials,
Ascoli Piceno 1993.

Balducci,
I primi passi
(First steps),
cement, wood, and leather,
Montecatini 1993.

Samuele Mazza for Pompili,
Caterina (Catherine),
wood and brass,
Florence 1992.

Maraolo,
Credevo fosse amore
(I thought it was love),
glass, leather, and flowers,
Naples 1993.

Pancaldi,
Pavoneggiarsi
(Strutting her stuff),
leather and feathers,
Bologna 1993.

Donatella Pellini,
Missing shoes,
resin,
Milan 1990.

Mario Bologna,
Luxury,
satin, spangles, and
leather,
Riccione 1970.

Yves Saint Laurent,
Strati
(Layers),
leather and rubber
Paris 1990.

Armando Pollini,
La molleggiata
(A spring in her step),
leather, spring, and
wood,
Vigevano 1980.

Emilio Cavallini,
Globetrotter,
leather and rubber,
Pisa 1990.

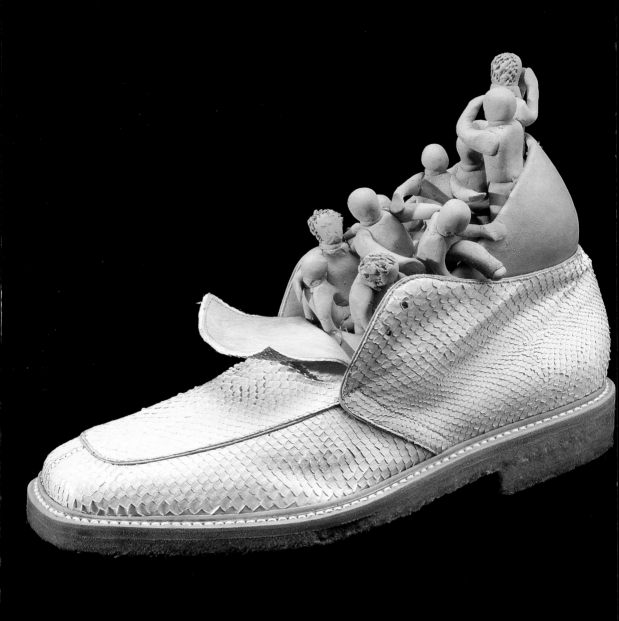

Luciano Landi for Borri,
Scarpa affollata
(Shoehorned in),
leather and terracotta,
Florence 1993.

Lorella Zappalorti for Kidland,
A child can be the killer,
leather, mercury, Plexiglas, and
condoms,
Prato 1993.

Giuliana Signorini for 3A
Antonini-Lumberjack,
Di figlio in padre
(Father and son together),
mixed materials,
Florence 1993.

Nando Muzi,
Madrepatria
(My country),
fabric, wood, and satin,
Ascoli Piceno 1993.

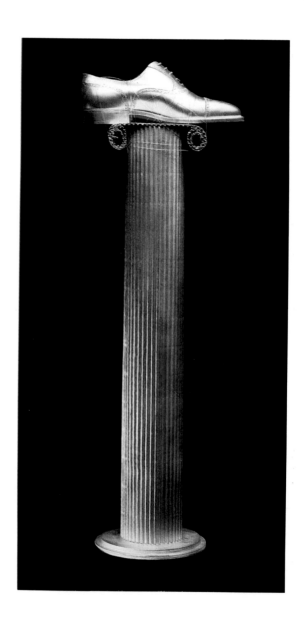

Nenad Jovanovic' for Barrett,
La classica scarpa
(Classic shoe),
leather and cardboard,
Parma 1993.

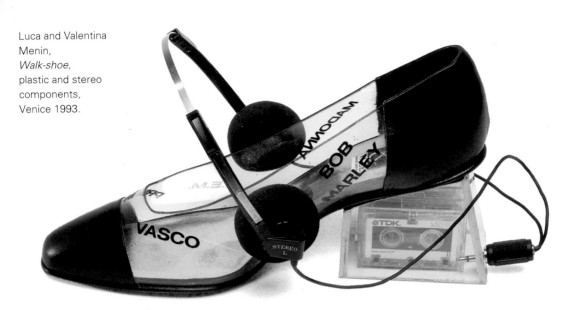

Luca and Valentina
Menin,
Walk-shoe,
plastic and stereo
components,
Venice 1993.

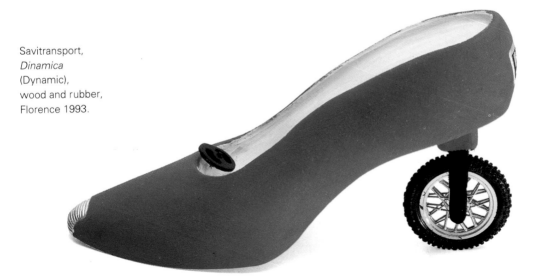

Savitransport,
Dinamica
(Dynamic),
wood and rubber,
Florence 1993.

Jimmy Baldinini,
La gatta sul regno che scotta
(Cat on a hot tin tiara),
mixed materials,
Rimini 1993.

Samuele Mazza for Di Brera,
Zeppa
(Elevator shoe),
fabric and cork,
Florence 1993.

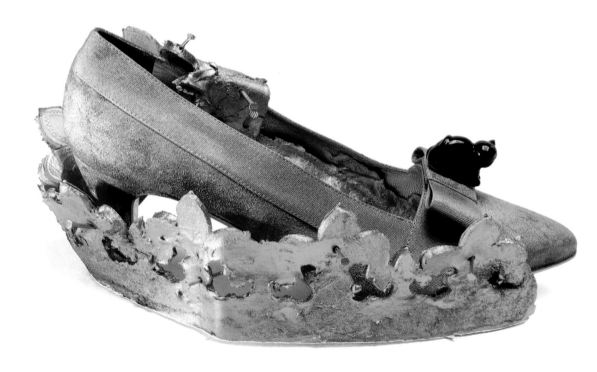

Gianna Meliani,
Ndebele,
mixed materials,
Pisa 1993.

Robert Clergerie,
Optical,
leather and plastic,
Paris 1993.

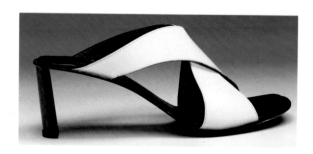

Tokyo Kumagai,
Up and down,
suede,
Tokyo 1980.

Martin Margiela,
Porki's
(Porky's),
leather,
Paris 1992.

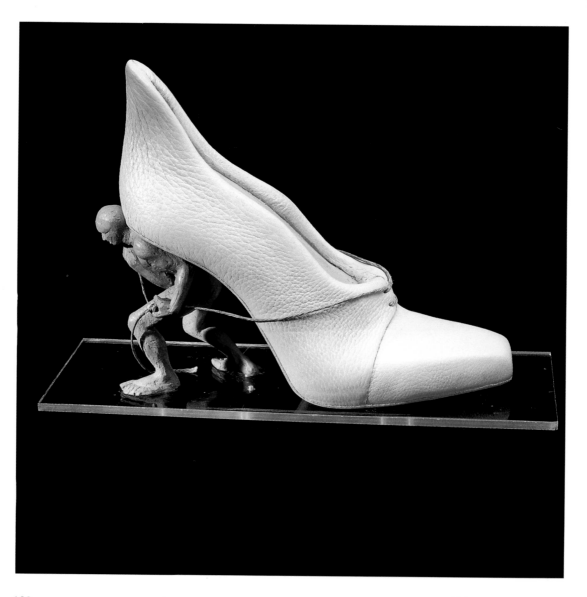

Samuele Mazza for
Bamar,
Antaeus,
wood and terracotta,
Florence 1993.

Arman,
Memories,
Collection Doris Montajes Venet,
patinated bronze,
New York 1991.

Laura Cardillo,
Diamonds are the Girl's Best Friend,
strass and filigree,
New York 1993.

Federica Marangoni,
Ciao Bella,
Murano glass,
Venice 1990.

Steven Lowy,
Sohonderella,
mixed materials,
New York 1993.

Vincent Gargiulo,
Gemini,
leather and wood,
New York 1993.

Diego Dolcini,
Dalí,
leather and wood,
Bologna 1993.

Giuseppe Zanotti for Casadei,
Colata
(Stream),
steel fluid net,
Rimini 1994.

Mario Valentino,
Venus,
coral and wood,
Naples 1954.

Lelas Goran for Sergio Rossi,
Colazione da Tiffany
(Breakfast at Tiffany's),
suede,
Milan 1993.

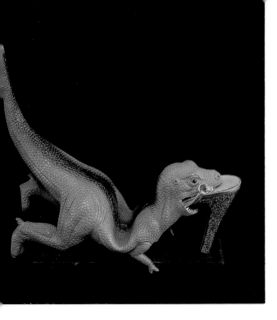

Nicola Salvatore for A.N.C.I.,
Jurassic Shoe,
plastic and wood,
Como 1993.

Nicola Salvatore for Armando D'Alessandro,
Squarpa
(Shoe Attack),
leather and wood,
Como 1993.

189

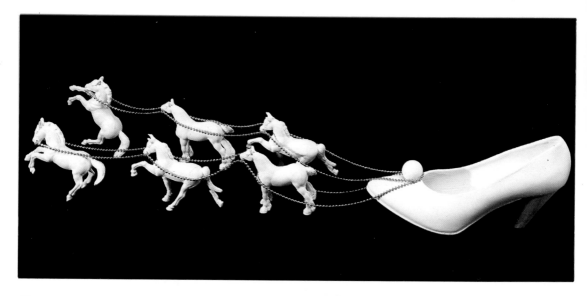

Giuseppe Di Somma,
*Mezzanotte
(Midnight),*
plastic and leather,
Florence 1991.

Bettina Werner,
*Deserto rosso
(Red Desert),*
coarse salt, wood, and plexiglas,
New York 1993.

Michael Celentano,
Mother Nature Shoe,
wood,
New York 1993.

Lisa Corti and
Angelo Barcella,
Gabbietta
(Cagelet),
Milan 1993.